AF260731

Gary Popejoy

3

The Blind Man,

Big Man and Silver Fox

The Blind Man
Big Man and Silver Fox

James G. Popejoy

On the Patio, Under the Umbrella

A pact of three Jackals, from a variety of economic and social situations, they strive to expose the truth.

They practice camaraderie with those who laugh or do not.

Gary Popejoy

Self-published

Gary Popejoy

In
Memory of

Mel (Sam)

A colorful figure, a guy of laughter.

He has moved on to inspire, joke,
and laugh with others.

1935-2019

Gary Popejoy

Dedication

It is a pleasure to dedicate

The *Blind Man, Big Man and Silver Fox*

To

Everyone - Everywhere

The Blind

To the many who lead monotonous lives, in the hopes they

experience the delights and dangers

of an adventure. Open up, see others with open eyes and share

with those:

Who cannot see?

To all seniors, their children, and grandchildren: Give insight into

the Young's future.

To loving children, beautiful grandchildren, and

A Devoted Wife.

Thank you for understanding the intentions

of writing this book.

Gary Popejoy

Table of Contents

Big Man and Silver Fox		5
Dedication		9
Table of Content		11
Preface		13
Acknowledgments		15
Introduction		16
Chapter 1	Starters	21
Chapter 2	Who's Who	27
Chapter 3	The Patio	34
Chapter 4	Repeat and Repeat	42
Chapter 5	Salsa and the Refrigerator	50
Chapter 6	Gossip File	60
Chapter 7	Top Secret	69
Chapter 8	The Cane	83
Chapter 9	Salsa Girls	94
Chapter 10	Crazies	106
Chapter 11	Tomorrow	124
Chapter 12	Fallacy	137
Chapter??	Superstition	148
Chapter 14	It's a wrap	156
The Author		167
Book Titles		168
Author's Last Page		169
Advertisement		171
Notes		172

You can't deny laughter;

When it comes.

It plops down in your

Favorite chair

And stays as long as it

Wants.

Stephen King [1]

Preface

The Blind Man, Big Man and Silver Fox is a compilation of stories from many different chats while sitting around a patio table— under the umbrella—at a senior living center. Bob, a blind person, and Guillermo, a cook, encouraged author Gary Popejoy to create an exciting book of life from those fifty-five-year-olds and older. This book is molded using stories contributed by seniors of various backgrounds. This mixture of stories and events evolved into an amusing assortment of real-life drama.

This book has something for everyone: adventure, gossip, humor, mystery, and romance. These stories are observations from seniors who have *lived* the parts.

Does it have both personal truth and little white lies?

The Blind Man, Big Man and Silver Fox are a pack of three guys from different economic and social situations who practice something important: fellowship. The three men sit sipping wine, diet soda, and eating cheese and crackers with barbequed hotdogs while doing what they do best: Reminiscing. These three (some call Jackals) hope to open seniors' eyes about *themselves* while at the same time bringing humorous laughter and insight into what comes to everyone in 'later life.'

Please laugh with those who laugh or make those who do not laugh at least smile.

Gary Popejoy

*In
Memory of
Mel (Sam)*

A colorful figure, a guy of laughter.

*He has moved on to inspire, joke,
and laugh with others.*

1935-2019

Acknowledgments

The Creators and Author acknowledge each contributor however trivial or copious in speech or ideas. From spoken words to those written allow others to feel fellowship and friendship with unity in the different lives of seniors.

Thanks go to those who laughed and contributed to *The Blind Man, Big Man, and Silver Fox.*

Martha M. McLaughlin; thank-you for the friendship, time, and editing skills performed.

Tony Farentino, for his edits, advice, recommendations, and patients. Illustration, page 148 is awesome. Thank-you.

Robert Torres for his wonderful illustrations in this book.

Robert Seijas, Pete Carrisosa, and Gilbert Simons great inputs. Thank you for being an individual of fun and suggestions.

Many thanks go to Addie for her continued encouragement in writing this book and others.

To all seniors near and far, have fun in your Golden years?

Introduction

One day while sitting around a table, Bob, *The Blind Man* and Guillermo a *Big Man* and cook asked Gary the *Silver Fox.* "You are retired, a traveler, an airplane buff, done clandestine military things, and an author." As an author of two exciting books, one about the melting glaciers of Alaska and the other about Buddhist temples of South East Asia. Write an inspiring book about seniors for seniors that creates excitement about fifty-five-years-old and older seniors, for seniors? Also, make it an eye-opener for others to learn seniors' ways.

Wow!

The Blind Man, Big Man and Silver Fox became a compilation of stories from many chats while sitting around a patio table under an umbrella. The enlightened stories did not occur or happen in one day, or night, but months and years from seniors who lived the parts.

There is something for everyone: adventure, gossip, humor, mystery, and romance.

It has personal truth and little white lies!

Seniors are a wealth of knowledge and facts with experience, education, successes, fast track living, homeless encounters, business start up's and failures. Seniors have had marriage successes and disappointments, ups and downs with children, divorce, and death. Seniors are ready to share their stories.

The Blind Man, Big Man and Sliver Fox

In this fifty-five-years-old and older senior housing complex, medical problems become a way of life, while living expenses continue to rise.

So, who do they share? Do they go to their neighbors? Cannot bother them! Do they go to the local cocktail bar? Not a good idea! If they see something and tell someone, are they called a gossip?

In these chapters, seniors' share humor and identify situations: good or bad. These stories of gossip, habits, and behaviors show how little things can make a person happy or sad.

Here is a glimpse into the life of seniors.

First! Is this book going to solve problems (maybe)? Is this a seniors' self-help book? The author does not think so but believes it should promote laughter. These stories clarify shyness, attitudes, success, and failure to create laughter, intrigue, and suspense. Other seniors' truths and disappointments may cause readers to think about their situations?

Many may wonder, and ask, who and what do seniors and gossipers talk about? Some: the military, where they were born and how they arrived here at Valley Oaks Place, VOP. Many talk medical issues, and who sang what during Karaoke. They address their humor and sadness to others who live in the midst of many. Politics, let us not go there and the children.

These stories will cause wonder, laughter, and hopefully make some feel better. One paragraph could ignite a lightning strike in one's imagination. That single occurrence could change an attitude to make one share with others or get something off their chest!

Join the journey and enjoy *The Blind man, Big Man and Silver Fox* by Gary Popejoy. It should make readers feel better; after all, others' hardships and experiences sometimes make other problems seem small to meaningless.

Many of our younger generations sidestep seniors who are their parents and grandparents. Why? The younger generations are building a career and family of their own in this fast-paced world. They live and depend on the two paycheck system; some work two jobs and do not have extra time to share. Other siblings are caring and nurturing their senior loved ones.

*In this book!

*I am going to show you!

*This book is going to solve?

See how some seniors share with others as this book strives for humor by identifying situations: good or bad. The stories of gossip, habits, and verbal behaviors show how little things can make a person happy or sad.

Three old guys Bob, Pete and Gary (some call Jackals) desired to enlighten seniors, parents, and siblings' with knowledge about seniors and senior life. The cast of three sat reminiscing each other's past.

What do gossipers talk or say? Oh, Boy! Politics? Let us not go there. They do discuss the military, medical issues, and who sang what during Karaoke — many consider the humor and sadness of those who live in their midst.

We sat outside the clubhouse at a patio table under an umbrella and talked. The discussions developed into this manuscript: *The Blind Man, Big Man and Silver Fox*. These enlightening stories did not occur or happen one evening, or night, but throughout months and years.

These stories will hopefully encourage laughter and make some feel better. Readers will learn something from others experience. One paragraph could ignite a lightning strike in one's head. That one act could change an attitude make one share with others, or to get something off their chest!

One who waits to read this book will be days behind in senior life-learnings. Every day one fails to enlighten through *The Blind man, Big Man and Silver Fox* causes continued 'Senior Moments.' Alternatively, many may fail to realize that other seniors are similar.

The Blind Man, Big Man and Silver Fox are a pack of three from a variety of economic and social situations. They strive to expose the truth by practicing camaraderie with those who laugh, and those who do not.

Join the journey and enjoy *The Blind man, Big Man and Silver Fox* by Gary Popejoy. It makes others feel better—after all, others' hardships sometimes make personal experiences seem small to meaningless.

The

Blind Man,

Big Man and Silver Fox

Chapter 1

Starters

V*alley Oaks Place* or VOP is a senior living complex for 55-year-olds-and older residents located at the southern end of the Santa Clarita Valley (SCV). Recognize SCV as a suburb of Los Angeles. It is the home of Six Flags Magic Mountain theme park. The William S. Hart, Heritage Park locals, call *Hart Park*. It is the backyard of the historically preserved home of William S. Hart (1864–1946), a colorful western cowboy, silent film actor, screenwriter, director and producer during the late 1910s and early 1920s. Santa Clarita is full of historical significance: Stagecoach robberies beginning 1874 in the Newhall Pass. The 1842 *Placerita Canyon Gold Strike* at the *Oak of the Golden Dream*. The March 12, 1928 bursting of the 185-foot St. Francis Dam, to record-setting wildfires consuming thousands of acres of lush mountain scenery.

There is *Vasquez Rocks and Nature Center* created 25 million years ago by an earthquake along the San Andreas Fault. Natures formations named after, a notorious California Bandit, *Tiburcio Vasquez* who used natures creations to elude officials, 1873-1874. The rock formations today are seen worldwide in many Hollywood movies and commercials.

Back at VOP, it is no wonder some people believe VOP stands for *Very Old People*. Others believe or think VOP as *Very Odd People*. Maybe there are both which is OK. It is like *VOP's* for *Vibrant Outstanding* and *Proud* where talkative conversationalists are known for their *logic and wisdom.* Some call VOP *Very Opinionated People.*

Nevertheless, VOP consists of seniors', some who hide their griefs and fears. Most are looking for peace in their declining years. VOP's residents are older, single, divorced, or widowed. Some individuals and couples live at VOP to save on expenses. It is a diverse ethnic mix of post-retirement, retired and downsizing seniors' who want to enjoy their golden years in peace.

Here at VOP, strangers adopt strangers as friends who communicate exciting stories. We meet a neighbor on a pathway leading toward the clubhouse, mailbox, coffee pot, or trash receptacle. Some walk for exercise, while others exchange words of wisdom.

"Hello George, how are you doing?"

"Hi, ah! Strange, cannot remember! What was the name? "

"That is ok George. It is Gary."

George continued, "Oh! That is right, Gary. Today at the doctor's, the nurse extracted blood and took my blood pressure," then said, "take this investigational drug." It seems every time I am at a doctor; they give a new prescription. The doctors work for the pharmaceutical industry to make extra money—for themselves—off us the patient."

George, "Be careful, take a deep breath. The doctor knows what he is doing."

"It was a she. Good looking, this time," George added."

On that note, it was time to say, "See you later, George."

In the VOP clubhouse, on the activity room's bulletin board, there is an incredible number of written restrictions. These rules management imposes on residents and guests are for our protection, they say. Some residents, with or without dementia, are afraid to enter the clubhouse to get their mail. They cannot remember what to do or not, so they gather their mail and go.

On Bingo or Keno days the same twenty-fifty players arrive with their quarters and sit in the same seat they call *mine or theirs*. They play, wait, and hope to hear themselves call *Bingo!*

A potential winner excitedly raises their hand, Bingo, then have their card checked. The Bingo checker calls, "Winner." The winner then receives a prize. A sigh is heard from the crowd, "Boohoo!" Then a new game begins.

Now mind! Bingo has rules! Those not playing Bingo must be quiet! When encountering a friend at the water cooler, coffee pot or mailroom, the players recommend Bingo onlookers *whisper*. To enjoy watching television, turn the volume down and hearing aid up.

Do not disturb the players.

Why? Guess! They are concentrating and need to hear the Bingo caller call "B-8" even with the turned-up loudspeaker—the same speaker which notoriously upsets Non-Bingo players.

Does it bother those reading in the library? Yes, it does!

On one occasion Mrs. Army and I sat near the mailroom discussing the Salvation Army. She is a retired employees who happened to be hard of hearing. Our voices raised and became louder than usual because the Salvation Army lady kept saying, "Speak up."

From somewhere the Bingo Cop, Mrs. Sumo her nickname, shouts "Be quiet! No one can hear the Bingo Caller!"

Next, from nowhere, face to face, Mrs. Sumo stared me eye to eye. She commanded, "Stop talking." Still, face to face, she stomped her right foot down hard on the floor, shaking the walls.

The Bingo Cop, Mrs. Sumo, is reprimanding us for talking. WOW, what a cop!

The *Bingo Cop* continued; first, she scared the Salvation Lady to tears. Then the *Bingo Cop* swiftly turned her mean-looking face—square jaw—, beady eyes—, and large caveating flame-shooting nostrils toward the Silver Fox.—She placed her club-size hands on her hips and grunted loudly, "Now Be Quiet!"

An inability to stay quiet is one of the conspicuous failings of humanity. [3]

Walter Bagehot

Mrs. Sumo turned a military about-face. She quickly marched back to her Bingo cards before B-8s called.

One may ask? Did we lower our voices? Yes! We did.

Now during Bingo and Keno days (twice a week) not to offend players, non-bingo players retreat to the outside pool area—our oasis under the umbrella. We non-Bingo players have a good time talking and listening to others, tell stories and hear the latest gossip.

The Blind Man, Big Man and Sliver Fox

The Big Man, Guillermo, a professional cook loves to BBQ. So a couple of nights a week the BBQ gets fired up. We have a potluck dinner that brings people and chit-chat; he makes our ribbed meals great!

In the comfort of the day or evening, we sit, deliberate, and try to solve world problems. No politics. These patio chats bring a wealth of opinions, even from Bingo players! Some tell a story, make a statement, or ask a question then merely leave—usually without an answer.

We found these seniors are like many—the weather seems to affect aches and pains. The majority of residents have lived here for several years and enjoy the life it presents. The oldest person I have known here was a single woman, 101, who lived with her dog—Flex.

9-1-1 is the VOP number called when someone oversleeps or has not been heard from for an hour or two. Thanks go to the paramedics and fire department for their excellent and tireless work.

Yes! Independent VOP seniors are like many other seniors in the community where the weather seems to affect aches and pains.

So why

Do seniors live here?

Their independence

Chapter 2

Who's Who

The tall, muscular stranger wore distinguished dark-colored glasses and a tailored suit. He appeared to be in his late sixties or early seventies. He appeared superficially poised and confused as he faced the elevator door. His actions seemed odd; his left hand searched for the elevator buttons? *Something is not right here. What is his problem? Moreover, why is he there?*

Looking closely and watching for unusual movements, something is close to the stranger, along his right side. He held whatever it is lengthways semi-hidden. *Strange? What was he hiding or trying to protect? Was it a concealed weapon? A baton? Maybe a baseball bat to use as a club?*

What-ifs raced around this thick-headed healthy worrywart. What if this is a *new resident,* okay. What if *he does or does not know something from the past?* What if *he was offended for some reason?* What if *the CIA, days are catching up?* What if this is *a hitman?* What if there is a *contract out on the Silver Fox?* All the questions remained unanswered.

The stranger quickly turned. We are now facing each other. The thin stick-like weapon about three-and-a-half to four foot long came into view.

Alert! Quick, the tense body formed a defensive walking posture. Slowly I slip my right hand into my jacket pocket, and firmly grasped a roll of quarters I obtained from the bank, moments before. Am I ready? *Yes! I am primed for action.* Just then I thought of the Beretta pistol locked in the safe box. My heart started to pump faster than its regular beat. Am I ready for action? I asked again.

Do not stop, or he will get suspicious! I continued slowly forward toward the stranger. Barely passing him at the elevator, the object along his side believed to be a weapon, came into a less hidden view. It was long, thin, and white with something round at the bottom. *Strange!* I thought.

The stranger raised his left hand upward toward his face; he then shifted his dark glasses upward. A look at the tall man's face and into his eyes that told a sad story. The hand fumbling, fashion dressed stranger-is blind!

Still cautious, I slowly approached the six-foot, 220-pound stranger. "Are you having trouble? Do you need some help, sir?"

The blind man tells me more about himself. "I live on the second floor, which *oversees* the swimming pool area. I cannot find the right button for up." the stranger said in a soft-spoken voice,

"It has Braille text next to the different buttons," I suggested.

"Thank you, but I have not learned the Braille language yet," the blind man said.

Being cautious: I helped the stranger understand the elevator keypad— primarily where the up/down and floor buttons located.

Inside the elevator, I explained and guided the blind man's hand to the second-floor button and let him push it.

As the elevator door was closing, I quickly expressed myself to the blind man, "How about *overhearing* the pool activities? Not *overseeing* the swimming pool."

The blind man laughed and said, "That is good. Moreover, thank you for your help."

I turned and walked away.

I did not reply but went directly to my apartment. I retrieved my house key from under the flower pot where I keep it. I opened the door, went inside, turned on the television, and fell asleep in the recliner.

Nothing else exciting came of the casual meetings today. I felt today was the same as yesterday and will probably be the same tomorrow.

I have seen the blind man pass my apartment as he walked toward the swimming pool and spa on several occasions. He sits in his darkness under an umbrella. For hours he plays his music and talks to whoever stops to say hello.

The day, like yesterday, was drawing to an end. The sun sinking behind the trees that shaded the swimming pool—as they cast their shadows, the air temperature dropped quickly. I would have loved to swim in the large pool, but my body does not handle the cold water very well these days. I do soak in the spas' warm water with its jets blowing hot bubbles on me daily. The water helps me relax before I fall asleep.

Working at my computer, I noticed that darkness had approached. The decorative light illuminated the big tree outside my window. At

10:00 PM, the security guard will turn the clubhouse lights out unplug the two coffee pots, regular and decaf and then lock the doors.

Most seniors at 10:00 PM locks themselves in their apartments until morning. Some go for late-night insomnia walks. Others take the dog out for its last trip to the dog park for the evening.

By 5:00 PM daily, I go to the clubhouse and the mailbox to pick up my unwanted mail. Usually, I enter through the automatic double doors. Every day I notice two large trash receptacles full with delivered and unsolicited mail that's thrown away.

What a waste of a beautiful shade tree, I thought.

I walked into the mailroom and opened my mailbox door. I retrieved my daily publications, bills, political flyers, and other junk mail directed toward me.

Just as I locked my mailbox, the light in the room seemed to dim. I stood still and rolled my eyes upward in puzzlement. *Why?* I turned toward the door and was astonished to see a gigantic figure, more prominent than Mrs. Sumo. This significant, massive figure of a man stood at the entrance of the door where he blocked the light from entering.

The *Big Man* ducked under the open door header and stepped into the mailroom. Filling the mailroom, the giant stoods before me, in a green t-shirt with gray shorts, completely healthy; aside from his massive frame.

My first reaction was to think of NFL's William "The Refrigerator" Perry, a 450-pound former American professional defensive lineman during the 1980s and 1990s. If not the man himself he could pass for the former giant football player in size.

Holding my mail, I timidly said, "Hello."

In a low but heavy voice, the Big Man said, "You are the Silver Fox I hear people talking about?"

My eyes bulged open! *Silver Fox!* Only a few know about that nickname.

I was surprised by the question. Gossip, real or false, flies quickly in these senior living units. I assume many have little to do but exaggerate. They begin to believe fantasies—then spread the fake news.

Surrounded by mailboxes, one small window, a single door led into the mailroom where movement is blocked by this bolder of a man, I said, "Excuse me, big guy, I am late and must go." I squeezed between *The Refrigerator* and the mailboxes.

Once outside the mailroom, I headed straight to my apartment.

Crossing the patio getting nearer the back gate, I hear a voice coming from a patio chair. "How is Miss Thailand? Does she feel better today?"

"Yes, Albert," I said without missing a step to the back gate.

I noticed that the "B" building apartments' glass door was left open. I shut it again! The management rules include: *Keep all doors closed. If the public doors open, close them. After 10:00 PM lock them.*

Inside my apartment, thinking of the Big Man, I opened the refrigerator door to get a diet soda—no more alcohol. I've been dry for many years, at my wife's request. Now I have the dreaded disease of diabetes, and even my doctor says, "No more alcohol."

I can sit in my reclining chair, look out my window and into the garden. The large tree is beautiful with mysterious shadows that move and twist in the branches. Decorative lights shine, bringing life to the many shadows that represent my past. Soon I see the dark branches change into a dizzying array of dreams, ideas, and memories that include an elephant, praying hands, a cow with horns and a baby chicken. Harden combat soldiers hide and move around in the tree branches. As gentle winds sway the branches, soldiers perish.

Comfortable and relaxed, I start to doze into the twilight zone. My eyelids fluttered open, then closed repeatedly. My mind wonders: *What will tomorrow bring?*

My eyes settle into the closed position. Finally, I am asleep.

Morning brings a new perspective to the tree that begins to shade its peaceful surroundings from the hot sun

We Gather Together

Socializing on the patio

expressing feelings

Chapter 3

The Patio

The blind man passes my window on his way to the patio, swimming pool, and spa. He will sit in blindness under the umbrella talking with those who stop. When he returns to his apartment, I notice how he places his walking stick in front of him to guide his travels.

How and when did he go blind? I wonder.

The day is drawing to an end. The sun is sinking behind the trees which shade the swimming pool. Trees cast their shadow, and the temperature drops quickly. I look forward to soaking in the spa to rid the body of its senior aches and pains. I want to go to the swimming pool. *Why don't I?* Simple, temperature. The water is too cold; my body's metabolism does not adapt to the cold water like it once did. Management says the pool is heated. It may be ok for the younger generation of swimmers but not for an older adult such as me. For example, when a teenager, wow! That was the life—surfing in the Pacific Ocean, at Newport Beach, in fresh, enjoyable ocean water. Temperatures hovered around 58 to 60-68 degrees. Now that I'm a senior, it may be the mentality, a generation gap, or whatever, but the water is too cold now!

I was thinking about the day. I had been to the gym, pressed my make-believe 100 pounds, been to the spa, taken a nap and now headed to see if the United States Postal Service delivered (pulp cut trees) to my mail, yet. Oh yes! Will I see the walking refrigerator in the mailroom?

Outside near the swimming pool, I can hear Samuel the happy Chinese, United-States Air-Force Vietnam-Veteran Pilot. Getting closer, I can understand, see, and hear Sam for short. He is sitting at the patio table, laughing his hardy *"Ha, Ha, and Ha's!"*

Sam is known for his laugh. One sentence or comment and he lets out his loud *"Ha! Ha! Ha!"* While he laughs, he swings back into his chair, flinging his hands high over his head. His actions are different and unusual; everyone agrees.

Sam and I spend several hours discussing the wars: WW1, WW2, Korea, Vietnam, and the current conflicts. We exchange our accomplishments and failures. To me, Sam is a man of unscientific, non-technical, methodical myth, of both earthly and unearthly questions! He enjoys the television program "Aliens," and he smokes other people's cigarettes and drinks their beer when he can. He utters to everyone that his pension is low and that he cannot afford where he lives—even with a roommate.

Sam is talking, telling, and maybe discussing a new phenomenon he uncovered on television about *Black Holes* in the Universe with our friend Albie.

Albie, an older gentleman, older than Methuselah, is always around. Methuselah is a "man of the javelin" or "Man of Selah," a biblical patriarch and a figure in Judaism, Christianity, and Islam who is said to have died at the age of 969. He is the longest-lived figure mentioned in the Bible. Our Methuselah, Albie, sports an uncombed head of white hair—which he would try to cut himself every couple of months. Everyone believes Albie has *Dementia*" and is known in the complex by some as the *"Do you like it here?"* senior from Manhattan.

Younger, Albie graduated from New York University with a degree in communication and journalism. According to Albie, he had an excellent career as an employment headhunter in New York. He knows his theaters, where they all are, who played them, and has seen all the great plays along Broadway.

Now he lives with his wife of many years here at VOP. She moved here to be close to their children and grandchildren, bringing Albie along.

In the Club House, I poured a cup of decaf coffee. It is a good thing I was in the Army and learned to drink black, thick coffee, twice and three-times overheated: with coffee grounds. Coffee is free for the resident's—complements of management.

Once again, it is time for Bingo, the favorite pass time for about sixty avid players.

"Hi Elaine, any luck?" I whisper.

Elaine shakes her head, left to right, meaning no luck—yet.

Barb sees me, winks (she winks at everyone) and turns to the caller's voice when she hears *"B-8."* She has four cards in front of her, hoping for a big win. One dollar fifty cents: the winner takes all!

Passing through the clubhouse to the patio—Maria, Mary, Nitnoi and two others see me and wave. I give a quick wave to each, acknowledging them.

Albie is sitting at the table quietly alongside the Blind Man, both listening to Sam tell a story of the aliens he observed in Alaska when stationed there.

Great, my introduction will be straightforward; I told myself.

Thinking of Kenny Rogers's song, *The Gambler* and remembering those lyrics: *Sitting at the table' reading people's faces.*

I chime in, "Hello guys, what-sa-up?" Then I ask, "Who is your friend?"

Sam answers first, "This is Bob; he is blind."

"Hello Bob, my name is Gary. I am the guy who helped you at the elevator a couple of days ago."

"Oh! That was you?"

"Yes, that was me." We then bump our fists together, acknowledging one another.

"Talking about the elevator, why do people not like elevator music?" I ask the group.

Albie answers, "It is not opera,"

Sam looked at Albie and said, "That is a lame answer . . . It is because they do not have speakers."

Bob interjects, "Why?"

"Guys, guys, guys, you can *surely* guess wrong . . . People do not like elevator music because at first, it is uplifting, but, at the top, it lets you down." I crack a smile, as I finish with the punchline.

Bob and Sam remark in unison, "That is a good one."

Albie is a harder critic. "You better not quit your day job."

The blind man's comment is more encouraging, saying, "Hey Gary, thank you. I was having trouble that day understanding the elevator."

Bob then surprisingly asks, "Are you the one they call *The Silver Fox*?

I want to think a moment. "It is Gary, the Author of 'Buddha and His Temples', and 'Meltdown'—a nice guy."

Sam blurts out, "He *is* the Buddha."

Albie counters Sam, "Gary has been writing a book about Buddha forever and a day. Well, in kind! He has finished one book in a series of three, so far."

"Thank you guys that is enough about introductions." I quickly interrupt before the older men continue with what they have heard. "Bob, I have to go. I am sure I will see you again soon."

I turn to Sam and Albie. "Guys be thoughtful in your words while talking about me to Bob."

I turn to walk away; I notice Rosberg, the man called 'Double-O-six point five,' coming through the door from the TV room in the Clubhouse.

Sam asks me, "Since you know a lot about airplanes and space I want to talk to you about 'Area 51', where they keep the Aliens the government keeps covered up."

"Later Sam, much later. We will talk." I shake my head. I want to flee this scene quickly. *'Of all places Area 51?'*

Who shows up at the table next but good old Albertus--Einstein as everyone calls him. In his right hand, he carries a small box wrapped in silver paper.

George is the first to ask, "What is in the box, Einstein?"

"I do not know George. *Now-and-then* I get these little boxes in the mail from *here-and-there.* I never know what is in them. *Sooner-or-later* I will open it and find out.

The Blind man asked, "Albertus, help! Can you explain *this-and-that?* I cannot understand what you are talking about?"

Albertus continues. "All right, *This-is-this,* and *that-is-that.* They usually travel as a team named *this-and-that* but never under the heading of *that-and-this.* It would confuse *those and them* who understand *this-and-that.*"

George, puzzled, and confused asks? "Mr. Einstein, let me understand. *This-and-that* is in the silver box *right-or-wrong?* Alternatively! Is it t*his* and not *that* or *that* and not *this?* Einstein, I am so confused, will you please clarify *this-and-that* and what is in *that* silver box."

"Ok! *Yes,* and *No;* this is why: *This-and-tha*t appear as they do and not what they can become with a simple switch to *that-and-thi*s, which is not generally accepted."

Albertus takes a deep breath mid-way through his explanation.

He continues, "*This* implies something is within range, vision, proximity, and nearness. *That* is something not within one's range of vision. Example; *this* would be *this* unopened gift received in *this,* silver box. *That* gift box contains *this-and-that* for the entire family or me? Once *this* un-opened gift is opened, the family gets a box of *that* that now reveals to be precisely *this-and-that.*"

"So! What is in the silver box, Einstein?" Albie asks again.

"I am not sure. It could be some of *that* because the last time I received t*hi*s type of box it had a little of *this and that.*"

Guillermo, nick-named Guille, AKA William finally remarks, "Einstein! You will not or do not want to tell us because it is a box with '*this,*' Prozac, or '*tha*t,' Horney Goat Weed."

Einstein laughs. "Maybe Guille, you could be '*Right-or-wrong.*' '*Sooner or Later,*' I will open the package and find out whether it is *This-and-That* or if it will be *That-is-this.*

What is in the silver wrapped paper box? *Good question.* We may never know what is in the box. It could be '*this,*' or it could be '*that.*'

You Cannot

Leave footprints in the sand

If you're sitting on your

Butt,

But then who wants to leave

Butt prints

In the sands of time? [30]

Unknown.

Chapter 4

Repeat and Repeat

Albie was sitting next to the coffee pot inside the clubhouse when I arrived to get a cup of 'Joe.'

Albie asks the same question the last time you talked to him. "Do you like it here? Do you plan to stay here? Why, do you like it here? Why? How come? And how is your wife?

"Yes Albie, I like it here. Like I told you before. I can lock my door and go anywhere at any time, for as long as I want. No lawn to cut, no house trim to paint, no tax and I am closer to the small town activity. Like I've said, I do not want or need the two-story house or want to climb another stair to a second floor. Albie, I do not want or need a large house any longer. My wife and I would use only the television room, kitchen, and one bathroom. We slept in one bedroom and closed off the other three. As I've said to you several times before— we downsized, to be here. Our small, cozy, senior cabin tucked away by the trees – and we like it just fine. I can write in peace. The trees, clubhouse, swimming pool, and spa give me a feeling of comfort, warmth, and relaxation. Ok? Do you get it?"

Once again, Albie displays that familiar blank stare.

"Albie, pay attention—friends I once visited, Susana and her husband, Loui, had a problem. He always watched the baseball game.

Susana, in her loudest voice, would say 'Loui are you even listening to me?'

Loui, a brilliant engineer, would say to his wife, 'Susana that is a strange way to start a conversation.' She threw up her arms and shook her head in wonderment. Louie did not blink an eye as he continued watching the ball game."

Is this relevant to the story? No, not really. It is, however, a thought which helps explain Albie and his repeating the same questions—over and over again.

I get up to leave. I ask Albie once again, "Ok! Dooo-yooou understand?

Albie responds, "Where are you going?"

"Outside to the patio, to visit with our new resident—the Blind Man."

I grab my second cup of coffee, plus an extra cup, and exit through the double glass door of the clubhouse. I head toward the blind man sitting in a patio chair under an umbrella talking to Anna and 'Double-O-six point five.

I approached the patio table and asked, "How is everyone?"

Anna and 'Double-O-six point five, say their greetings. They follow up with a friendly inquiry, "How is your wife?"

"She is being treated for cancer. She is exhausted, sleeping a lot but doing well under current circumstances. Right now, she is napping. Thank you for asking."

"So, how are *you?*" The two ask.

"Me, I am worn out from the daily medical appointments she must attend at 8:30 AM. Thirty-eight miles—one way, during the morning freeway rush hour on our commute to the Hollywood Cancer Center."

Bob, the Blind Man, offers his kind words. "Sorry to hear that Silver Fox. Send her my best."

"Thank you. I will, Bob; I brought out an extra cup of coffee. Would you like it?"

"Yes, thank you. That is kind of you."

Rosberg, Double-O-6.5, turns to Anna and says, "Did you get a cup of coffee? I did not."

Anna turns to Roseburg and replies, "No! And it does not matter. Gary had two hands and offered the coffee to Bob. If you want coffee go get it."

Double-O-Six point five called by some stands up quickly and remarks, "I have to go and watch 'Star Trek' in the TV room. Anna, do you want to go with me?"

With a sweet smile and kind eyes, Anna looks at 006.5 walking away. She whipped her sharp tongue and flung toward him. "No!" She turns toward Bob and me and says, "That man's crazy."

We agree with Anna! She smiles, turns, and walks to her home.

Bob and I are in general conversation talking about nothing and everything when Albie came to the table.

"Hi."

"Who is there?" Bob asks.

"It is Albie, the guy who cannot remember his last question—then turns around and repeats it," I whisper to Bob.

"Do you like it here?" Albie asks Bob, who did not answer. "Do you ever see couples or go to dinner with some of the guests here?" Albie anticipated the blind man's answer and responded for him, "No, why not?"

"Do you like it here?" Albie now asks me. He still does not receive an answer. "Do you ever see couples or go to dinner with some of the guests here?" Again, Albie answers his question. "No! Then, why not?"

"Do you like or ever go to the theater?" Albie directs his new question towards the Blind Man.

The Blind Man replies, asking Albie the obvious. "Did you notice I am blind? That I have a blind man's walking stick, painted white, and I cannot see?" Only a touch of sarcasm in the blind man's words. "Did you notice I play music? Do you *HEAR MY BOOMBOX PLAYING* and that I love to sing, play the guitar, and the drums?"

Albie turns toward me again. "Did you find a publisher today?"

I shake my head, left then right. "No."

Albie asks, "Why not?" He then changes the subject, as quickly as he asks. "Did you write anything about me today?"

"No Albie. If I did, you might not like it! So, wait until the book is published and be surprised!" I answer his question quickly.

"Do you like the theater?" Again Albie changes the subject. "How about Broadway? Do you know who starred in Cats'?"

"Sorry, Albie, I do not. I was exposed to girls, not to the grandeur of theater art. I love petite females with long wavy hair— auburn; charming smiles; and firm looking breasts; with a mature, well-accented, curved waist and hips. The one you call *Miss Thailand.*"

Bob quickly replies, "Do you mean Liza May Minnelli, the American actress, and singer? The Liza May Minnelli who received an academy award for her portrayal of Sally Bowles in Cabaret—who has a powerful contralto singing voice?

Albie tries to butt in once again. Everyone ignores him.

I would be lying if I said I was not impressed with Bob's knowledge of the theater, or Liza Minnelli.

The Blind Man ignores Albie and continues. "The Lady with a Quote!"

I've said it before, (and) it's absolutely true:
My mother gave me my drive, but my father gave me my dreams.
Thanks to him, I could see the future.

Liza Minnelli [5]

Bob started singing the lyrics to 'I'm losing my mind.' *I, I'm mm losing...!*

Abruptly he stops singing to ask a question. In a commanding voice while tapping his forehead with his index finger remarks, "Albie! There is a different version of the song that reminds me of you. Would you like to hear this new version?"

"Oh! Really?" Albie is excited. His eyes shift toward Bob. He tilts his head, pointing his left half-decent ear toward the singing Blind Man and says, "Yes."

"Here it is, the best I can recall. It is called, A *Lost Mind* by the Silver Fox:

> *"The sun comes up; I am at the pool, not thinking about you.*
> *The coffee cup spills, now I laugh at you.*
> *Go away before you cause me to lose my mind.*
> *The morning ends, he finally goes, I think about you no more.*
> *I talk to others, what a joy. I hope they know about you.*
> *I lose my mind when he's around.*
> *All afternoon I am not thinking about you.*
> *Or I would Lose My Mind."*

Albie is excited, "That is great!" He claps his hands together. He stands up, clapping all the while. A standing ovation—one could say. "When are you going to put it on a CD and give it to the world as the next number one Grammy?

"Soon Albie, very soon. We must first finish this book, *The Blind Man, Big Man and the Silver Fox."* I reply.

"Guys, I know what we should do to celebrate 'Albie' and this new hit. This Thursday, instead of taking our afternoon naps, we can join the *Wine and Cheese Social* in the clubhouse at 1:30 PM. We will sing this new, soon to be, hit song: '*A Lost Mind*' to our fellow Wine Tasters."

Every one sits stone-faced. Albie walks away—silent.

"It was only a suggestion," I added. "See everyone at the BBQ tonight?"

"Ok." Everyone responds at the same time.

"Goodnight," I reply.

The Big Man

Robert R. Torres

The Big Man, preparing the salsa

Chapter 5

Salsa and the Refrigerator

Guillermo walks toward the barbecue carrying a plate of meat. He places the platter of chicken and beef on the empty patio table.

The piano player (Bob) does not look at Guille or anyone else as he plays without sheet music. He sits upright with an expressionless face—tapping piano keys to produce a beautiful melody.

It is past six o'clock. Guille is standing alone at the Barbecue Grill cooking a meal for his wife and himself.

Bob, the Blind Man, stopped playing his piano keyboard. "Silver Fox, who is that I hear over there?"

Bob, it is the Big Man I mentioned to you. The Big Man, the size of a refrigerator, the giant I encountered in the post office the other day

"Oh, Guille," Bob said.

"Guille! What are you cooking, tonight, quail eggs or shrimp?"

"Neither, it is marinated goat meat, fresh from the local Country Market."

The big man placed his meal on the grill then sauntered over to where Bob and I were sitting. His body's frame, 6'-7" at about 400 pounds, blocked the sun's rays that flashed between the canopy foliage.

He lowered his large shell of a man filling the empty patio chair and said, "Hello guys."

I remarked with the expectation of being squashed flat. "Bob, Guillermo, is so big that he is blocking the sun. Can't you tell?"

"Not really, but if you say so," came from Bob in a loud and deliberate voice to ensure Guillermo could hear.

The Blind Man in a pleasant voice then said, "Guillermo do you know Gary, the *Silver Fox*? And that you blocked the light in the mailroom the other evening?"

"Oh! That was you. The one who squeezed between me and the mailboxes. Sorry if I frightened you. I was tired and not myself. Sorry again," the Big Man said.

I asked, "How long have you been here in this heavenly, high-quality, senior-living complex listening to the chatter and gossip?"

"We, Judy and I, moved here two weeks ago into the 'C' section."

Maria, 94 years old, sat listening to Bob play the keyboard. She still drives and walks two miles every day. She is quiet and reserved, but her words join the conversation. "I had a C-section 75 years ago, resulting in the birth of my Karrie Ann. She was a lovely girl who died of cancer! Oh, how I miss her!"

The table went quiet and numb with surprise. No one even let out a breath. Bob's blind eyes stared towards The Big Man. The Big Man's head slumped forward, and he shrugged his shoulders at me as I gazed motionlessly and went limp! Then I said, "Maria, I feel for your loss," I manage to reply.

Bob choked up, stuttered, and then changed the subject. "Guillermo is a cook and caters to customers. If you want something cooked, he can cook it."

"A Big Man like you? I would have thought you would be a football player like NFL's 'William, The Refrigerator' Perry—the 450-pound defensive lineman. You could pass for the former giant football player." I uttered.

Guillermo leaned forward in his chair and placed his left elbow on the table. Guillermo's chin rested in the palm of his hand with four fingers tapping his upper lip, muttering. "I never played football. I had a disqualification disease when I was young. And no military, they disqualified me for my size. I wanted to be in the Navy and see the world by sea. My father was a heavy equipment operator from Sedona, Mexico. My beautiful and wonderful mother was from Mexicali—on the border of Baja California and Mexico. Did you know most people in the United States do not know Mexicali is the capital of the state of Baja California? It is located directly across the border from Calexico, California. Anyways, my mom and dad met in the San Fernando Valley and married. I was born in North Hollywood. With the family, I moved to Sylmar, California, where I grew up and attended school."

Bob jumped in. "Guile, take a breath,"

Not skipping a beat or breath, and ignoring Bob, Guille continued. "My mother worked as a chef in the restaurant business and learned to cook gourmet dinner recipes at the finest restaurants. She passed many recipes to me. So I began catering over 30 years ago, to both small and large customers. I love to barbecue, and today I am cooking chunks of goat meat, marinated, with one of mom's recipes."

Guillermo continues with his life story.

"I had worked for the county of Los Angeles, where I retired early because of two heart attacks. My wife, she works to pay the bills these days. We have been together for thirty-five years, with one daughter who lives in Texas and works in the world of science and technology as a Bio Technician."

Again Guillermo stopped, got up from the patio chair, and walked to the barbecue to check his spoils for the night.

One by one, Anna, 006-and-a-Half, Mary and the others come to the table. Anna brought her usual Tofu and rice dinner. Double-O-6.5 or Roosberg arrived with an ice-cold Popsicle and sat down with us— nothing wrong with dessert first. Albie strolled out of the clubhouse with a cup of coffee and three cookies. Excitedly he told us a Good Samaritan left cookies for others on the marble countertop next to the coffee pot. Albie sat down next to Anna without a word. Soon the grill was cooking hot dogs, veggie burgers, vegetables, and the potluck tables were in full swing. Table chatter was wild, *Ha, Ha'* Sam brought a bottle of Cognac and shared with all. Also, several brands of beer bottles sat on the table, mostly empty. Others, like me, brought their brand of diet soda.

Albie asks Claud the truck driver, "Do you like it here?

"No," he said, "that is why I am moving."

Why don't you like it here?

"None of your business. For the others sitting here, wondering? I contracted as an office's operation manager for a large trucking company in Victorville, Ca. I will be coordinating the big truck scheduling and movement. Those Big Rigs you see on the freeways."

The day turned to twilight. Varying conversations continued to circulate the table. One by one the table cleared and the Pot-Luck Party-Goers retired for the evening. Suddenly 006.5 jumped up surprising everyone. He announced, "I am late. I must go to the TV room to see Star Trek. It has started, and I must go." Darkness settles in by 8:30 PM this time of year. Most people go to bed between early evening and ten o'clock. It must be past Albie's bedtime as he sat dosing and dipping his head, being quiet for a change. Somehow the quietness must have awakened Albie. His head popped upright, eyes opened, and he said, "I have to go home. It is late."

He got up and left three of us sitting talking about the Refrigerator's five Spice Girls.

Guillermo, Bob and I were holdouts who continued talking.

"In my youth, girls were everything. Party was the game, rock and rollers were in, and Pot flowed freely. At home, I made great tamales, which I sold on the street or catered. I also made salsa that everyone liked. I still make and sell great salsa," Guillermo told us. "I would make a few dollars, get loaded, wake up, and start over. Later I started cooking my mother's recipes. Once I received an order for a case. That is twenty-four bottles of salsa! I was jubilant! That is when I began word of mouth selling my catering and salsa earnestly."

Bob and I were happy to hear Guillermo's story and said, "You should continue to make your salsa and market it as '*Spice Girls*.'" We began saying girls' names at random. Bob then started to sing the lyrics of *Maria* from the *West Side Story*. He stopped singing and started to hum the tune, 'I met Maria, A most beautiful girl,' or something like that. He then added, "Yoho, I am from East LA and Guillermo's from Sylmar. We better pick another name closer to home?"

Guille said, "Molly?"

"Yes! Yes! Yes! Perfect," I said. "Little Richard—*'Good Golly Miss Molly.'*

"It could pass?" Bob said.

One by one from Guillermo's party days and the spiciest girls he knew, partied with, dated or laid beside, emerged memories of those younger days.

Albie sat listening to the conversation then chimed in with his wit. "The Spice Girls are an English pop group from the United Kingdom who were famous in the nineties. Their names are Emma, Geri, Mel B., Victoria, and Melanie C." Albie's weak voice faded with the words, "They were outstanding!"

Bob quickly said, "Albie, did you ask them if they liked it here?"

Albie, barely awake, replied. "No, I did not get to talk to them when they were in New York at that time. At the!" Albie paused, "At the time," another pause, "where was that?" Puzzlement came over his face as he tried to recall his thought. He paused, looked at me, and asked, "How is Miss Thailand?" referring to my wife of fifty years.

"Just fine," I replied.

"How is her . . . ?"

Guille cut Albie off, suggesting, "We should not use those Spice Girls' names because of copyright and all that stuff." Everyone agreed!

One of us asked Guillermo, "Who was your first date? Give us all the low down dirty little secrets or mysterious details you remember?"

He looked up into the canopy foliage, rolled his eyes up, and explained, "Ah! I was sixteen, so that would be *Sofia*."

A grin formed on Guillermo's face as he reminisced.

"Sofia and I would sit on the sidewalk curb for hours talking about life: running away from home, sailing the world in a private boat together. When we could muster up a few bucks, we would sit at our special place on the sidewalk and smoke a joint together. One unfortunate day, her father was arrested for hit and run. Sofia and her mother both returned to her grandmother's house in Texas. The dreams we fantasized together never happened."

I looked at Bob and said, "That is the first name of Guillermo's five bottles of Salsa—*Sofia!*" I then googled the I-Phone and found Sofia. "The origin is Greek and means 'wisdom.' Yes! She was wise to get out of Dodge before her best friend Guille could corrupt her. Bottle one: *Sofia, Spice Girl Salsa*, pictured in Spanish clothes sitting on a curb."

"Great," Bob said. "Who was the second hot mama Guile?"

He answered very fast, "That might be *Maria*. I met her at a party. We were stoned sitting on a couch. She leaned her head on my shoulder, and soon, we both passed out."

The Big Man formed a big grin on his face.

"Morning arrived early. My head felt like it was in my back trouser pocket. I looked at Maria. She was gorgeous. Together we wandered hungrily outside where I pointed to my Tamale Cart. It was still parked where I had left it. We sat on the curb and ate Hot Tamales together. After some small talk, we slowly pushed the food cart along the street together."

Guillermo stopped and looked into the sky. He continued, "Guys, I want to tell you, Maria was well curved, fine breasted and her voice was soft and sexy. She was my unexpectedly wonderful dream girl. She smiled a dreamer's smile. But horror struck my inner soul as I said, "Maria, you have a beautiful smile with a black bean from the Tamale on your front tooth." I then mumbled the words, *"Stupid! Why did you say that?"*

She rolled her tongue over here teeth and said, "Thank you, *Guillermo,*" like it was nothing. Then she asked, "Does it look better?"

We approached the corner where people gathered waiting for their morning commute. From nowhere, out of the blue yonder, her beautiful voice opened with these words:

"Hot Tamales!

Hot Tamales! Anyone?

Get your Hot Tamales here.

They are Hot like me,

Fresh and hot like me,

Hot Tamales anyone.

Tamales, just like me, so good.
Sorry no cherry today, just Hot Tamales.
Get your Hot Tamale today.
Hot Tamales."

"We became friends and together sold Tamales by the day and partied by night. We buddied together for a while, having fun—smoking Pot. I could never get to Home Plate, let alone First Base with her. She was waiting for the right time and the right guy. We continued to sell Tamales until one day she disappeared. Where? I do not know; not even today do I know where she is."

Spice number two: *Maria, Spice Girl Salsa.* A quick google found Maria—Spanish for Mary, with many Italian meanings: "Beautiful," "ransom," "virgin," and "merciful."

We argued the name. Guile, he wanted "virgin," Bob wanted "Mary," and I wanted "Maria." I told them both, "I am the Silver Fox and am typing the story—it will be *Maria!*"

There was silence. After a short pause, I said, "Make up your minds. I am going home. See you next time. Good Night."

Bob asked, "What about the other 'Spice Girls,' Guile must tell us about?"

I chimed in. "Bob, did you ever hear that there is always time. Better yet, Benjamin Franklin's statement, '*Take time for all things; great haste makes great waste.*' Bob, there is always tomorrow."

"Goodnight, Silver Fox," Guillermo, the Refrigerator, said.

"Goodnight, 'Big Man,' goodnight 'Silver Fox,'" The Blind Man added.

"Goodnight," I replied.

We departed going our different ways. With good luck and great prayers, we will see each other tomorrow.

Chapter 7

Gossip File

There is not much to see inside the security fence and gates around this senior living center. No flower garden, the grass has been removed and replaced with compact dirt. Yes, I said dirt: Earths soil. To make the landscape more active and exciting management placed a few large rocks in the dirt pile.

So, what we hear, all the gossip that is spread during Bingo, Keno and at the mailroom, makes up for it. Here on the patio, under the umbrella, we listen to it all. It was said by the French Journalist Antoine Rivarol, "Of every ten persons who talk about you, nine will say something bad, and the tenth will say something good in a bad way." [6]

During Tuesday's Bingo recess Wanda said, "Did you hear Poison Ivy, (Brenda) the 62-year-old has been sneaking over to Carl's apartment?

Maria asked, "Do you know what they were doing?"

"Well. *You know.* You know what I mean. I am sure."

The senior complex gossiper Wanda replied.

One sweet voice chimes in, "Poison Ivy and Carl—the retired movie stagehand who can hardly walk to his mailbox?

Fat Carl?" "No way. Impossible!" Another person speaks up.

Wanda defending herself replied, "That is what I overheard Elaine and some other lady talking about while I was waiting for the elevator."

A Giving Prayer:

Please help those lonely people who think overheard voices are the truth.

Give them help to remove their sharp tongues.

Eight women sitting in the clubhouse cutting newspaper coupons, one said, "Did you hear management told the lovely lady in building 'B', the one who makes beautiful potted flower arrangement? Don't feed the birds and the squirrels?

The manager then gave Ms.? a letter to discontinue supplying and feeding the critters or leave VOP?"

"Why?" Asked Carla.

"Well, you know . . . Mrs. Who Ever is not supposed to feed the animals. Everyone knows that. It was the lady who lives on the second floor above her who alerted the office. The office manager (no longer employed at VOP) loves to write discharge letters, you know." Wanda said

Wanda continued, "Did you know Russel is in the hospital for a hip replacement?"

"No way," said several ladies at the same time. "I saw him get a cup of coffee this morning.

He was walking just fine," burst out Bernice.

"Well, that is what the brown-haired middle-aged girl in building 'A' told me," Wanda remarks.

Harriet cut in, "You mean the thirty-five-year-old Brenda, who is not 55 yet, the one who should not be living here in this facility for 55+-year-old gossipers?"

"Yes, that one," Wanda replied.

I asked Wanda, the gray-haired lady from Chicago, "Gossip, is that what your life has come to?"

Walter Winchell told his audience on his hit radio show long ago: *"Gossip is the art of saying nothing in a way that leaves practically nothing unsaid."*

Speech, both in truth and non-hurtful way, comes from the power of the mind. To separate fact from untruths deserves proper respect. *Right Speech* means to avoid harsh, obnoxious words, idle gossip or false storytelling/backstabbing—most importantly not to tell lies. *Correct speech* refers to everything we say verbally. All speech cultivates in our mind: positively or negatively, about what we think of ourselves, and ultimately, what we choose to say and do in this world. Incorrect or wrong talk: frivolous speech, lying, gossip, swearing, are very unproductive dialogs that hurt people. Words do tremendous damage when spoken incorrectly. Gossip and spreading untruths can ruin marriages and careers. It causes sleepless nights, heartache, and indigestion!

It would help when you talked if you would not convince someone of Fantasy or False action as real. When it is a lie. It is perfectly fine to live in a fantasy world, but someone who wants to persuade others of untruths need more wisdom training

— Buddha

"Communicating in thoughtful ways, unites and heals people bringing them closer together. Therefore, one must cultivate speech that is clear, truthful, and compassionate" — an excerpt from *Buddha and His Temples-Fifteen in 37 Kilometers*, by Gary Popejoy (2018).

I stepped out from the swimming pool and strolled to the patio table with five chairs and an umbrella. After moving a chair into the sunlight, I plopped down to dry my wet body.

"Hello, Gary. How are you?" a voice at my backside said.

I turned and saw Dave approaching. "Hi, Dave, how are you? You need a swimsuit to take a dip in the pool. The water sure is nice today."

"No swimming for me," Dave said. "I did come to ask you a question. I heard you submitted to become the Resident Council President this year. I know on other occasions you were asked and always refused."

"That is right, I refused. I do not want to be president of a bunch of whining; gossiping crybabies scared to walk to the office and file their complaint. When some complainers asked, 'Why not submit your claim yourself?' They, the office personnel, say something approximating: 'If we complain anymore we may have to move.'"

"You never will be the person you can be if pressure,
Tension and discipline are taken out of your life." [7]

James G. Bilkey

"Dave, do I believe the office said that? I am sure of it. You know, I prefer to help individuals that come to me. I listen, give guidance, or refer them to where they can get help."

Dave responded, "It is a rumor going around now, and I know you know it is time to elect a new Resident Council President.

Gary, if you change your mind and decide to run, I am behind you."

"Thank you, Dave, but no thanks." I continued to bask in the sun.

The double doors of the clubhouse swung open. Out popped Sam: 'Zip-A-Dee-Doo-Dah Zip-Pa-Dee-Yea.' "Did you hear? Did you hear? Carol, the weird girl, accused Bill B. as a sexual predator! Carol was in the TV room when Bill B. made a pass, trying to put his hands on her!"

Dave and I simultaneously said, "Bill B.! No way! Not Bill B."

Sam repeated three times, "Yes, really it is true, Herb told me!"

"Sam, stop! Listen! Herb is a boozer. He makes up stories and spins tales. You do know that, don't you?" I tried to interject some reason.

"Well yes, but, he said it is true." The jubilant Sam said.

"No Sam, if true the police would have been here and arrested Earl. Everyone would start gossiping about him and her as soon as the police arrived—Sam, I ask you, did the police come and arrest Earl?"

"No? I do not think so! I am not sure."

"Sam, instead of watching Space Aliens and UFO Conspiracies on the television for your up to date information, know that those television programs become scripted for profit. Also please understand that gossip, idle talk or rumors, especially about personal or private affairs of others is scandalous. It is also known as dishing or tattling. Whatever it is called it's gossip."

Sam shrugs his shoulders at what I say. Did he understand?

"Sam, the next time you hear a story think of Socrates, the Greek Philosopher, who challenged others by testing them for gossip before he discussed the personal business of others by someone else."

The following is from *Inspirational Stories* by an unknown author, January 17, 2014.

'In ancient Greece Socrates was reputed to hold knowledge in high esteem. One day an acquaintance met the great philosopher and said, "Do you know what I just heard about your friend?"

"Hold on a minute," Socrates replied. "Before telling me anything, I would like you to pass a little test. It is called the Triple Filter Test."[8]

Triple Filter?

"That is right," Socrates continued. "It is best before you talk to me about my friend, it might be a good idea to take a moment and filter what you are going to say. That is why it is called the triple filter test. The first filter is the Truth. Are you sure what you are about to tell me is true?"

"No," the man said, "Actually I just heard about it and . . ."

"All right," said Socrates. "So you do not know if it is true or not?"

"No, I do not know!"

"Now let us try the second filter, the filter of *Goodness*. Is what you are about to tell me about my friend something good?"

"No, on the contrary."

Socrates continued, "So! You want to tell me something bad about my friend, but you are not certain it is true? You may still pass the test because there is one filter left: the filter of Usefulness. Is what you want to tell me about my friend going to be useful to me?"

"Well, no, not really!"

Socrates concluded, "Well if what you want to tell me is not true, not good, or even useful, so why do you tell me at all?"'

I then asked Sam, "Sam, do you understand Socrates' test?"

Sam sarcastically remarked, mocking me. "Sure Silver Fox, everyone knows about that old man Socrates and his philosophies."

"So! Sam, why do you spread such lousy gossip?"

"What gossip?"

"Now, let us examine the truths of the gossip we heard about Poison Ivy, The Bird Lady, and the hip replacement."

Sam shrugs.

"Poison Ivy, (Brenda) the 62-year-old has been sneaking over to the large man's apartment. That is true; Brenda did go to Earl's apartment! Brenda went to see Earl three different times at his request. Twice on Monday and once on Tuesday. Brenda is a retired electronic installer from a large company. Earl, with a new television, had issues and needed help installing. It required three visits to Earl's apartment to fix his Television. If a payment is required and it was whoop-pee that is their business, not mine. From the TV problem to sneaking into a man's apartment? That is real gossip."

I let Sam think about my words a moment before continuing.

"The beautiful lady in 'B' building who feeds the birds and squirrels every day? She received a letter from management to stop or leave. Right or wrong, yes or no?"

"Well . . ."

"Management did walk from the front office in building 'A', through the clubhouse, down the walkways to where Lady 'B' was removing dead leaves from her patio garden. The landscape gardener had neglected to do an excellent job, so Lady B was doing it for him.

"The Gardener?"

"Exactly . . ."

"With a new *lease* in hand VOP Management sought Lady B. They find her cleaning weeds and leaves from her apartment porch. "There was a transfer of papers from management's secretary to Lady B."

They *thank* her for signing up for another year and scheduled a free carpet cleaning in two weeks—*Karma* for helping to clean up after the busy gardener. Karma is the Asian thing—do well, and you will receive goodness in return?"

Sam blinked.

"The gossip! Wrong, once again. Just like Russel being in the hospital for a hip replacement. Wrong! Russel went to see his friend George in the hospital who is having *his knee* replaced. Russel wanted to give encouragement and friendship to George before his operation. George is 71 years old with no family, living on social security benefits—alone. Russel, the Good Samaritan, is wrongly accused. Gossip, go figure!"

0-2 for old Sam.

"Then, Dave heard I submitted to become the Resident Council President. Wrong!"

0-3

"Truth: I was not approached nor asked to run for President this year. It was the current President running against herself. She must say something to justify her running. It is my understanding that not many care for her. I am not sure I care for her…yet. She will become elected with one vote— hers." Only an assumption.

.

"I do believe the resident council is a good thing. It is the escape some residence need. For me? I enjoy sitting at the patio table, under an umbrella, listening to these and other stories coming from the enriched seniors who want to share."

Chapter 7

TOP-SECRET

For Your Eyes Only

Silver Fox

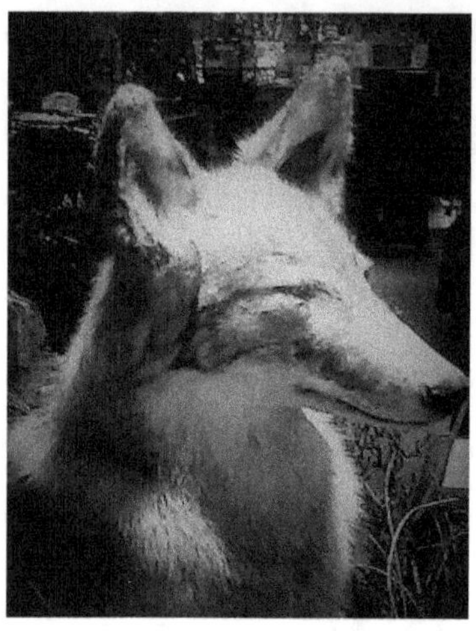

James G. Popejoy

The Silver Fox?

Attention!

To the Ladies and Gentlemen, Boys and Girls, Baby Boomers and the Millennials or Echo Boomers of all ages and ethnic backgrounds. The stories you continue to read or hear are real, exaggerated, and somewhat embellished.

Tun Ta-dun Tun

Tun Ta-dun Tun, TUN

The musical tune is similar to the television stories of Dragnet.

It was Donut Day, Friday, 8:10 AM, residents begin to arrive for their weekly donut and coffee treat.

The first to arrive at the clubhouse are Ron and his wife, Karen. She is known as the red-headed Bobcat. They are always early and sit at the same table—next to the coffee pot. They are a happy couple, even with their medical problems. Ron, is the unofficial Coffee Cop who reports: "Coffee, It is Hot," "coffee's cold," or "coffe is ok now!"

VOP management donates six to eight boxes of mixed glazed and sugar donuts, along with bagels, to the clubhouse every Friday for residents to enjoy. Some residents wait patiently, others impatiently.

It is a friendly gesture' I wrote in my notebook.

Donuts are picked up from *Jim's Donuts* our local Donut and Bake Shop. It is a public rustic-looking building tucked in the corner of a small shopping center. *Jim's Donut* is an excellent option for locals picking up a 'dirty dozen' or more that taste excellent.

Coffee and donut hour starts at about 8:30 AM.

Someone hollers, "Carl, you are late!" Carl arrived at 8:32 AM. He does not answer the two-legged badgers. He merely places the pink boxes of donuts from *Jim's* on the black marble counter top, opens their packaged lids then departs without comment. Poor guy!

The first persons in the donut line grab at their favorite sugar-coated or colorfully sprinkled donuts. Some heartlessly grasp to seize donuts: taking more than one, two or three at a time. Often they get ridiculed by other residents with comments comparable to save a dozen for my family who is coming later.

Others are waiting for inline comment, "Glad you could make it, Carl."

Our table countered the ungrateful with, "Thank you, Carl."

Double-O-Six-and a Half quietly approached the counter and selected a bagel. After spreading cream cheese, he toasted it in the microwave. With coffee and bagel, he joined our table. He says to us, "Donuts are not good for you, too much sugar."

The tables vary in size and gather mostly the same set of people to discuss any business that has occurred since last Friday. I think they call it coffee clutch: same people, same tables, and the same complaints. Often they are with comments along the same line as: "Save a dozen for my family, they are coming later."

"You are supposed to take only one, two if starved with a sugar attack," words of wisdom from our table.

The quantity donut taker brings a plastic box, chooses what they want, leaving none for late arrivers—without a care for others. We noted: this is selfish.

The same four ladies crowd the counter together. "I am the first." Then another lady, "No, I am first!" They place their walkers and canes to block others from getting in front of them. They want to secure their donut selection.

Men join the table and discuss 'guy' things. They talk about anything to nothing: from 'A' in Acura and cars to 'Z' in Zymurgy, a branch of applied chemistry that explains the fermentation processes in brewing, winemaking, and distilling. Have a beer type of thing.

When politics creeps into the conversation, it is not a pretty table — too many misfortunes have happened. The collection of egomaniac friends, therefore, refrain from politics.

Military, on the other hand, everyone has something to say— even the non-enlisted.

Our undercover donut patrol and surveillance continued until 10 o'clock. Our report compiled the following:

Coffee. It was cold. The Donut man plugged in the coffee pots to warm it. The donut poacher did not notice the pot was unplugged. This, understandable because they are complainers, not doers.

Donuts arrive plus or minus two to five minutes before 8:30 AM. Normal.

At the time of donut delivery, the room gets verbal. The donut deliverer gets abused by greedy residents wanting their share of donuts. Unacceptable.

Greed. At the front line—70 plus year-old women catfight to be first. Fun to watch.

Numerous residents appreciate the delivery. (The delivery person ought to stay and interact with the guests as they did in the past. Things are not like the old days.)

Some brought a plastic bowl and took more than one donut home. Selfish, greedy, and unacceptable.

All Donuts disappear by 9:15 AM. They lasted longer than anticipated.

Some guests came late and immediately left without donuts.

After donuts, most people would go home. A few will migrate to the patio to exchange personal stories.

Observation:

> *"That man who lives for self alone,*
> *Lives for the meanest mortal known."* [9]
>
> Joaquin Miller.

Surveillance concluded. Now what? Sit on the patio under the umbrella? Good idea.

The first to arrive on the patio to report new gossip was Sam. "Hi, guys. Does anyone have a cigarette or beer? Ha, Ha, Ha." He flops into a chair, throws his head back, and laughs again.

Our response: "No!"

Sam, our resident fighter pilot, watches Friday night movies of Rambo or some other action flick. Somehow Sam becomes the story, and his adventures resemble these shows. He turns into Rambo, Sgt. Ryan, Chuck Norris, and Steven Seagal, or some other movie make-believe warrior.

Sam does not realize we have seen the same re-runs to pass our evenings.

One day the discussion was Air America and the secret war in Laos, specifically my responsibilities. My electrical radio communication department—air and ground—installed tactical air navigation systems, Tacan, used by both civilian and military aircraft. It provided pilots with bearing and distance (slant-range) to ground or ship-borne station. It aided flight navigation and non-precision approaches to short landing fields hidden in the bush. The Tacan we installed was used to direct a significant number of the B-52 Strategic Bombers to rain down explosive bombs, written propaganda, and perform individual raids on Hanoi during the "Vietnam conflict."

Mille broke in, how long have you had your bird and how is your wife." And, all the other questions talkative women have to ask.

"Thank you for asking. My wife brought the bird home as a six-week-old baby—twenty-six years ago."

Millie spoke again, "Your bird told Hector, the maintenance man, 'go take a bath.' Hector replied; "later when I get off work."

"That is our bird. Hector is not the first person Choke Chi told to go take a bath, get lost, or sing Tina Turner's song *What's Love Got to Do, Cluck, Cluck* to."

The Blind Man, Big Man, Albert, Claude and I sat continued talking our subjects under the shade of the umbrella.

Albert asked, "How is your wife, Miss Thailand?" then, "Did you ever take her to dinner at the English Fish-&-Chip Pub?"

"Yes Albie, It was a few years ago. I told you."

"Did you like it?"

"No! I did not like it. I had told you that before."

"Why not?"

"It did not represent England, Australia, or New Zealand's style: neither their fish nor their chips. My family and I have lived in those countries, after all. Therefore, we have never gone back to that restaurant."

Claude, an Ex-Vietnam Navy Aviation Mechanic, stationed on an aircraft carrier in the South China Sea, sometimes further north to the Bay of Tonka, asked, "Silver Fox, how did you get involved with Air America?"

"It is a long, boring story."

"Then the short version, I would like to know!"

"Ok. I completed a classified assignment in the Army and did it very well. My Commander received a request for me to go to Saigon and report to Mr. Cumming, the station manager, for Air America.

Once at Air America, I trained several mechanics to install a new classified radio in their helicopters. Why? So they could communicate with other military services. It was a success, and I was offered a job to stay. Instead, I went back to my unit in the central plains of Vietnam. After my tour of duty, the Army transported me to Pleiku Vietnam. I and 200 others GI's boarded our plane for home. Glory, Glory, Glory was my feeling.

When the plane lifted off the runway, all the troops applauded.

After landing the military, transport C-141, 200 soldiers and I walked to the Duty Officer who assigns us to our new duty station or discharge point.

I was employed with EG&G and transferred to Mercury Nevada's Area 51. At Piute Flats, my colleagues and I installed specialized electronic equipment to monitor the exploding of Thermal Nuclear devices: bombs.

Mr. Dawson, President of Air America—Washington D.C.—called and arranged all necessary paperwork for me to report to Air America's Taiwan headquarters. Later I traveled to Bangkok and eventually to Udorn, Thailand, where I was assigned supervisory responsibilities for the Air and Ground Electronic systems. Eventually being promoted to Superintendent of Air Craft Maintenance."

"Ok, that is neat," said Claude.

Sam cut in. "I trained pilots."

We started talking about the FBI, CIA, Home Land Security, Border Patrol, and other security services and problems. Then the political crap started flying.

I suggested, "Let this new brand of terrorist in and you will have your grandchildren in rehab or dead! The terrorists are only a footstep away. Mix them with our own out of control gangs and liberal teachings, then be prepared to get the B' Jesus scared out of you!" The more cynical and nasty talk continued.

We continued through the night, trading our old war-stories.

I commented, "Guys, this is a fact. I have to go home because I have a big day tomorrow—and I am tired."

"Just one more story Silver Fox," Guillermo said. "Tell us about that infiltrating bad guy you had mentioned!"

"Ok, one more . . ."

Spy Games

Some years ago, I was in the jewelry business with my wife. It was just after ten in the morning when the telephone rang

"*Hello*, Addie's Gold & Jewelry, this is Gary, how may I help you.'

"Gary, this is Allen, from Alpha-One-Charlie."

"Allen, it has been a long time! What did I do to receive this phone call? The last time we talked was in Seattle at the Air America reunion."

"Yes, I remember, that was quite a party. It was good to see all the guys once again." Allen continued, "I am in Santa Clarita, your city, and need to see *you*. It is essential and affects *you*. I expect to see *you* at the Hyatt Hotel for lunch at one o'clock. We will talk more then"

"One o'clock It will be." and I hung up the phone.

Old memories started returning one at a time. Questions came too: Why me? Why now? It has been 30 or more years since I was involved with the military, CIA, Air America, and my responsibilities with the Secret War of Laos. I was sure it was not my affiliation with Area 51, Lockheed or the Skunkworks.

Allen was head of security for Air America, an excellent manager, and an overall good guy. We had often gone out drinking together after work. Our wives were not the best of friends but respectful to each other because of our job positions.

A quick shower and change of clothes, and I was off to the Hyatt hotel, about five miles away. I valet parked stating, "Keep the car close, in case I have to leave in a hurry."

I saw the door to the Hyatt Hotel automatically opened, allowing me to enter. I walked toward the front desk. Bearing over me to the right were two enormous sized elephants emerging between vases of bamboo. They appeared to be guarding the restaurant's entrance.

In the corner with his back to the wall, away from any low windows, was Allen.

He stood up and waved me over to the table where he was sitting. We greeted each other, shook hands, then sat down and ordered lunch. We both asked about each other' wife and children. Our kids went to the Air America School in Udorn, Thailand, together.

"Allen, I have to ask before you tell me anything: Who do you work for? Air America is an inactive unit."

I was expecting the FBI when he said, "Home Land Security." He then showed me his badge.

"I am impressed, Allen!"

"Gary, I want to alert you about that Laotian- who was a Vietnamese spy you stopped—before he could sabotage one of our communication centers. By the way a great job you did!'

"Yes, I remember him, the one that almost cost me a leg. The talented electrician I almost promoted to line lead-man—just before I caught him with his hand in the cookie jar of explosives."

"Yes, that one. Well, the little bastard has escaped Thailand's jail system and we understand he is traveling towards the United States. How, or where he will enter, we are not sure at this time. We do know he never did want to cooperate and has caused many problems in prison.

One man from the thousands of detainees—now *thirty years* later, he continues to hold a grudge. Something he never got over with, the war. It sounds like he is on his original mission that moved from Thailand to the United States."

Nervous would be an understatement for how I felt.

"Gary, listen carefully!" Allen looked directly into my eyes. "This low life has threatened to harm, and kill, all of the people responsible for his capture. He is an evil person who we never did return to his homeland, Laos. We do not know where he is at this time. Here is the *last* most current picture of him. Today he is older of course, and we believe still dangerous. We have notified law enforcement here and all location agents of this person as '*Armed and Dangerous*.'"

"I am sorry to tell you this type of news." Allen also said, "Just keep your family close and safe."

"I do not engage with anyone now-days Allen—I keep my nose down and my business to myself. Coming home and getting shot five times was my wake up call."

"That is good, and we see you have installed security bars at your jewelry store entrance, after you were shot and lived, like a good soldier. That is all good and well. Keep your surveillance system up and running. Gary, if you think you see the little bastard, call 911— *before* you shoot him. Call this number and tell the dispatcher your code name and number. Tell them what you have seen or believed you seen. We will do the rest. Any questions?"

"This is quite a reunion. Thanks for the heads up. I hope you catch the trader soon in some other country or state," my throat quivered as I spoke.

We talked about old-times and finished our meal. Allen picked up the bill leaving a one-dollar tip. He was always a cheap tipper!

Three months later, I received a phone call from Home Land Security, Lieutenant Nuckum. Mr. Popejoy; The Vietnamese-Laotian spy and saboteur, had been captured at the Canadian border infiltrating into the United States. He was posing as part of a New York Red Cross exchange group. That is the last I heard of him or the incident. Case closed.

Claude murmured, "What a story! For sure it is true, you say?"

The Blind Man asked, "I want to hear about the five bullets you received?"

"I do not have enough time tonight, maybe tomorrow or the next day."

"Promise," Bob, the Blind Man, stated.

I started walking home and replied, "I promise, maybe."

The Blind Man

Robert R. Torres

The Blind Man, standing tall.

Chapter 8

The Cane

Bob, The Blind Man, had gotten up early and wanted to sit on the patio next to the swimming area to enjoy the morning. It was 8:00 AM, the security gate to the courtyard and swimming area was still not opened. 'Not again,' Bob must have thought. He turned walked away, tapping his cane in front of him and disappeared around the corner.

One may question, '*Do blind persons walk until they bump into something? Maybe they count the steps? How do they know where, and where to count when they have never gone before?*' However he navigates, he arrives at the clubhouse front door that opens automatically. He walks by the table and chair area where he participates in Karaoke, proceeds past the coffee pot area, and out the large double glass back door. Miraculously he navigates the patio without falling into the swimming pool or spa and locates a table with a chair where he will sit under an umbrella.

Bob begins to play his portable keyboard and sings silently so not to disturb some cranky, irritable, resident who allows their life to get stuck in medical complaints. They complain about kids with their grandparent's supervision having a good time swimming.

As a senior, I have medical problems. I take care of them with a doctor, not my neighbor. Between my many medical appointments; I stop, smell, and enjoy the roses along the way.

The not-so-nice lady turned to me and said, "I am not talking to *YOU!* There are no roses here, only weeds."

This lady, neither one of us knew grunted, snorted, and made unusual facial expressions turned and walked into the clubhouse.

Good both of us acknowledged.

Anyhow! The blind man navigates the morning without a guide dog or assistance from people, using only his white cane with red tip.

Cane! Now that is interesting. It is an aid for walking. A stick that is essential to blind peoples' personal life. It helps the blind to get around and keeps them from bumping into most things. Society now accepts people using a white stick with a red tip as being blind. Most people will give lee-way and assist the blind at a stoplight, corner or intersection, or helping if the person appears lost.

Bob on the outside is a happy, witty, joking person who once entered into the high society's upper-middle-class status. Today Bob struggles with blindness. He has been abandoned and left alone by family—those he helped build into financial stability.

You see! Bob can't. His life began in East LA. His father is from Madrid, Spain and his mother from Nogales, Mexico. They met, married, and started their family-raising Bob, an older brother, and two sisters. Bob's father died from drowning during a fishing trip when Bob was four years old. The family lived in Boil Heights, a section of East LA, where he attended Bishop Mora Salesian High School, an all-male Roman Catholic school.

You remember the story of Cheech and Chong, born in East LA. Who argued birth vs. immigrant, citizenship, or green card? Is Bob's East LA the same as Cheech and Chong? I do not think so.

Bob, mesmerized in thought, continued to play his keyboard said, "My mother, a single parent, was very protective of her children. She sheltered us from the many evil environments that surrounded our neighborhood. As a child and young man, I missed out on many adolescent and young adult activities because of here over protection. I will say living a protective life sucks. I did not have many friends. My longtime friend is Johnny, whom I have known since the first grade.

One bright sun shining morning Johnny, a celebrated comedian, and musician, came to visit Bob at his apartment here at VOP. Soon they migrated to the patio.

"Hello, Bob. Who is your friend?" Someone asked. "Bob, come over here, you must sit under the umbrella, and join this rag-tag few and tell us who your friend is," Guillermo, the Big Man, asked.

Both men joined the ragtag few and began enjoying the company of each other.

Bob proudly introduced Johnny to everyone. "Johnny is my best friend. I have known him since first grade. He is a musical genius who can play several instruments, arrange music, and sing. He can beat a set of drums creating great rhythms. He headlined many shows and performed on ocean cruise ship tours around the world!"

I asked Johnny about drums. "Johnny, if a person wants to learn to play the drums, how do you hold the drumsticks?"

"Good question," Johnny said. "I am not sure I know the correct answer. If the request is pressing, you can Google it on your phone, or ask KFC. The Kentucky Fried Chicken manager should be able to help you."

Laughter came from everyone at the table. Bob was laughing. "See he is witty, and smart, always with a quick comeback." With that, Johnny excused himself to return to his Hollywood home.

People joked, told stories, ate potlucks, swam, and went home. The next day life will resume under the umbrella.

****

That following day Bob and I were sitting at the patio table by ourselves. The Blind Man said, "Silver Fox, I want to thank you and Addie, (Miss Thailand,) both of you have helped me in many ways. Together you have helped re-establish my feeling of satisfaction. Gary, it was nice you guided me around the 'Cowboy Festival' where we met Johnny Crawford from the television series *The Rifle Man*.

A big smile grew on Bob's face. His eyes glowed with passion, as he spoke.

"I appreciate how you introduced me to the Veterans' Affairs Office who helped retrieve several of my needed benefits. It was such an enjoyable, fun, and refreshing time when you, Addie, Sherry, and I went to the Santa Monica pier to eat and smell the ocean air.

"Gary! There are many more times and occasions I must thank you, Gary. Again, thank you!"

"You are truly welcome. I think you should tell Addie yourself. In the meantime, I will tell her what you have said—it will positively boost her feminine ego."

The next day, tall dark and handsome Bob returned to the patio. He started talking, which he is not short on doing. "When I was young, I wanted more, what? I did not know." He palled around with a few guys. They had gotten him nothing and nowhere, and I managed to stay out of trouble. Then, "Alone one evening, I was jumped and beaten by the 'Boy's in the Hood.' It scared me good. The incident caused me to become a loner until one day in 1966, wandering the streets of Los Angeles. I peeked my head into a military recruiting office on Broadway in downtown Los Angeles. After a short interview, the recruiter noted I had skills where I could work in military courts. The short Sergeant spoke with different recruiters who determine the Marine Corp would be a good match for me. After thinking it over a few days, I told mother then kissed her good-by. I then kissed the neighbor girls (?) good-bye and enlisted in the Marine Corps."

Marine Corps boot camp is all it is hyped up to be. The training is rigorous training teaching recruits to obey rules and a code of behavior, I enjoyed it all.. Two weeks before boot camp graduation, I became ill and sent to the infirmary for two weeks, missing graduation. I received an option to retake boot camp starting in two weeks or be assigned to an active training unit. I elected Boot Camp. Bob is the *only* person

I've known who volunteered for boot camp—*twice*. He told us he did better the second time because he knew most of the training routines. After Military graduation, Private First Class Bob was assigned to court reporting training in New Jersey. He did well in the military court system and was quickly promoted to Sergeant.

With an Honorable Discharge, Bob returned to Los Angeles where he attended UCLA studying journalism. He roamed around, the streets of LA questioning himself on what to do. Eventually, his military training qualified him for a job in court reporting, with the Los Angeles Court System.

Bob continued to want more. He began forming his own company. From one man he built a business drafting reports for the courts. Clients included celebrities, big and small companies, and more. The business eventually supported thirty employees. He married not once but twice. Both marriages failed sadly. When Bob's son came of age, he joined the company as its CEO.

Bob's blindness started in early 2000. He could no longer adequately manage the business. The CEO son, took over becoming the swindling owner. Quickly the successful growing business began to spiral down and out of control because of the lack of good business ethics and a big head that caused the company to fail. Bob was forced to close his once lucrative business. Closure created financial hardships for himself and many others. In a short period time, he went from a Beverly Hills address to a low-cost living environment, and gang-infested neighborhood in the high desert (not VOP) of Los Angeles County.

Upbeat, he interacted with his new neighbors and the ladies. His charming ways and humor caused the masculine macho ego gang members to attack and cause this blind man trouble. Fortunately, his daughter, who would eventually abandon him, helped him move and sloppily organize his finances.

As of this writing, Bob, a blind man is at VOP—safe. These stories from The Blind Man, Big Man and Silver Fox come as we sit around the patio table, under the umbrella, talking. We drink cold water and diet soda while listening to each other. Bob attracts and entertains. Some days the talk is just unbearable with everyone babbling a different story, subject, or gossip at the same time.

This day the cane tapped the floor, and Bob gained attention from everyone present. He asked, "Did I tell you that Laura wants to be my caregiver?"

"Really! Are you going to take on her and her brother in your one-room apartment?" Sandy, VOP know-everything lady, spouted out. "You know she lives part-time with Greg, the 94-year-old man next door to you."

Bob, with a puzzled look of disappointment, said, "Really, maybe I better rethink the offer?"

Everyone agreed, "Yes, you better."

Frances said, "Bob, with minor finances as you indicate, if you live with Laura, you will soon have even less. The office will get upset and charge you a higher rent, for live-in help…. Laura, she will expect a higher than normal wage!"

That ended the evening. One by one, the lonesome souls went home.

Bob was sitting alone on the patio, playing his portable piano. Before it became dark, Bob was getting ready to return to his apartment. Just then, Kate and Karen arrived and escorted him home. The two ladies and Bob occasionally would sit, talk, watch, and listen to the evening news together. They will drink a variety of fine wines, eat cheese and crackers until late, about 9:30 PM. After enjoying each other's company, the ladies will go home.

The next day Bob is sitting alone on the patio playing his portable piano.

"Bob is the rumor true? Do you have a mongrel you hang and lay with?"

"Is that you Silver Fox?"

"You guessed it."

"No, this white cane with red tip it does not bark. I use it to walk and guide me along like a friend. I can also use this cane for protection by using it as an Austrian aborigine's blowgun by shooting darts at an adversary. I can fold it and make it into nun-chucks. If needed, I push a knife out the tip useing it as a spear."

Just then, Bob grabbed his cane and poked my stomach. Wow! No knife.

"Take it easy, Bob; you are not Spartacus or do not look like a wild jungle spear chucking expert. If you toss a spear at the enemy and hit him slightly, he runs away with your cane. You will be left standing, by yourself, lost in the human jungle of darkness without a cane."

"Good point! That is why they call you the Silver Fox," Bob immediately countered. "Did you hear?"

"Did I hear what? Another love story you fantasied?"

"Something like that, but this time Ava and I were at the drug store where we met Bill and his girlfriend, Emma. They told us about Doctor 'C' and Dick, the bartender.

You know Dr. C's office is across the street from Dick's bar, next to Mike's Pizza and Deli. For the longest time at 6:00 PM, the Doctor has crossed the road and went directly to Dicks Bar. He always entered the bar, sat at the same barstool, and ordered the same drink—an *Almond Daiquiri* with Almond shavings on top.

Visiting the bar was Dr. C's regular nightly routine.

The other day Dick was wiping a table next to the window. He saw Dr. C closing his window blinds and put up the closed sign. Dick wanted to surprise the doctor and decided to make an Almond Daiquiri and place it at his favorite place at the bar.

Dick freaked out when he discovered he had no Almonds. He quickly took some Hickory Nuts and made shavings to place on top of Dr. C's drink.

'Hello Doc,' Dick said.

'Hello Dick,' Doc said as he proceeded to his stool and sat down.

Looking into the drink that sat in front of him, a puzzlement of concern came over the doctor's face. He looked up at Dick, squinted his eyes, and asked, "Is this an Almond Daiquiri Dick?"

'No. It is a Hickory Dickory Daiquiri Doc.'"

No laughter heard.

" . . . So let us change the subject. Bob, did you hear the story *The Blind Girl,* in Moral Stories, where the Author is unknown? Here it is.

There was a blind girl who hated herself just because she was blind. She hated everyone, except her loving boyfriend. He was always there for her. She said that if she could only see the world, she would marry him.

One day someone donated a pair of eyes to her and then she could see everything—including her boyfriend. Her boyfriend asked her, 'Now that you can see the world, will you marry me?' The girl was shocked when she saw that her boyfriend was blind and refused to marry him. Her boyfriend walked away in tears.

Eventually, she received a letter in the mail, the message said, 'Just take care of my eyes dear.'" [10]

With happiness or sadness, the human brain on occasions reacts strangely as in the story of the blind girl.

Bob the Blind Man, fortunate or not, has been able to see but now he must put everything: colors, shapes, and faces into darkness.

Chile Pepper

Robert r. Torres

The Cook and Salsa Girl.

Chapter 9

Salsa Girls
Continued

It was the middle of the week, Wednesday. The ladies had departed to their respective in-coves for the night. The Blind Man, Big Man and Silver Fox were left sitting in the twilight of the evening on the patio at a table under the umbrella. There was no moon, but the stars twinkled high in the sky. Bob would usually have been home at this time. Tonight he wanted to hear more about Guillermo and the Big Man's spice girls.

Guillermo's refrigerator-size body filled the patio chair he was sitting said. "Not tonight guys, I am tired. *I wan-ta go home.*" He got up, stretched his arms high above his head, and said, "Goodnight."

Before Guille could stroll into and out the clubhouse and disappear for the night, we serenaded him with a song. *The Table under the Umbrella*, which echoed the skies. The Blind Man and I sang a modified version of Detroit City, by Bobby Bare. [11]

Last night I went to sleep in VOP
I dreamed about spice girls not the orange groves of Sylmar
I dreamed about mother, father, sister, brother, and spice girls too
I dreamed about Sofia, Maria, Lucia, Laura

also, Kathy; the Salsa Girls

Oh, how I wan-ta go home.

Guillermo; The Refrigerator, with his back to us, raised his right hand above his head and gave us a thumbs up (middle finger). The Blind Man and I looked at each other thinking: *Later, he will tell us.*

We returned to our apartment for the night to watch the ball game, fall asleep, and wait for the morning.

The next day no Guillermo. Days passed, still no Guillermo.

One day his wife came to the table to get away from Guile and the confinement of their room. We call it a case of apartment cabin fever. Mrs. Guille, Judy, told us, "After Sunday church, Guillermo became ill and developed a summer cold or flu bug and remained confined inside. He wanted me to tell you guys, 'Hello.'"

"Tell Guillermo to get better. We will be here, and see him when he gets well," the table muttered. *So, what were we to do? Wait some more! Yes, wait.*

It was on Friday. Donuts and Coffee were on everyone's mind. Donut talk turned to repeat conversations: same old discussion, at least with new gossip.

We were talking about Guillermo. Albie repeated, "I never saw a person that big." Right on cue Guille then entered the clubhouse and stood directly behind Albie.

"You are talking about me again Albie," Guillermo said, in a startling harsh voice to intimidate Albie.

Albie frightened himself, uttered, muttered and finally spat a squeaky voice out, "Hi Guille. Good to see you and feeling better? Why the black eye? Did the 120 pounds Judy put the fridge in his place again?"

"Oh, how funny," as he grabbed hold of Albie's lean shoulder muscles and laughed. "Not this time. I tripped over my own feet and hit the table where the lamp *was*."

"Was," said Albie. Then, "Do you like it here? Are you going to move? Where will you go? What will Judy do?" All questions Guillermo, and the table ignored—like usual.

"Sit down and tell us about your black eye in detail." I tried to steer the conversation back on course.

"No, I came to check my mail. I am looking for a catering contract for a church social. The theme: *Meet Me at the Gate,* an event to help the retired prepare for their senior years. It is a great program that draws lots of people. This year they want 80 pounds of Guillermo's *skinless BBQ chicken*. The church provides delicious potatoe and macaroni salad, pork and beans, carrots or some other vegetables.

Sam looked at Albie, who turned toward Guillermo. Sam asked. "Are we invited? What do they have for drinks or do we BYOB, bring your one bot...? A bottle, Sam stopped, paused, and then said, "Sounds like a great topic."

"Yes Sam, and take your little white uncombed-haired friend here with you." Guillermo squeezed Albie's shoulder again.

Guillermo continued. "I will be at the Bar-B-Q Saturday cooking. Guys, her name is Lucia. I will tell you about her."

Albie asked, "Who is Lucia? Your charming wife's name is Judy! Isn't it?"

The Blind Man said, "Lucia is Guile's new girlfriend. Do not tell anyone or Judy will get upset at Guillermo. Then you will be called 'Albie the gossip.'"

"Ok!" Then Albie raised his hand, with his right thumb and the first finger pressed together up to his lips. He placed his finger to his lips and gave the no-tell motion of, *my lips sealed*. Then said, "I will not say anything."

Sam went into his 'cannot afford it routine,' his car accident and rental car problem. All these subjects we have heard more than once. He saw Laura across the patio. He jumped up and ran outside to serenade, romance, or hopefully talk to her.

Albie got up and went to the glass door of the clubhouse to watch and to study Sam and Laura's actions. Shortly after that, he began to wander around the clubhouse jungle of tables and chairs, and finally headed home. I think.

Saturday, Guile was cooking more chicken then I have seen cooked at *El Polo Loco's* grill. His BBQ chicken smelled good as it sizzled on the grill.

The Blind Man asked Guillermo, "How about Spice Girl number three, Lucia?"

"Lucia was a big gal with a great personality. We became friends when we worked at the county hospital where we were clean-up custodians, janitors. We cleaned the floors, toilets, emptied trash, and all the other things custodial crews do. We worked midnight to early morning.

One raining night I gave Lucia a ride home in my black Ford pickup. She invited me in for coffee and cooked an excellent breakfast. I sat on the couch, closed my eyes, and fell asleep. Midmorning she woke me. I stood up, she wrapped her arms around me, kissed me, and thanked me for the ride. I started picking her up and driving her home daily. We became very close—intimate—and almost moved in together.

As we arrived at her house one morning, we observed on her front porch an uncombed, long-haired, dirty-clothed man. His smile showed a set of ugly teeth.

Lucia shifted and became frustrated sitting next to me. She quickly said, "Thank you for the ride, Guillermo. Now leave, before 'my husband' figures out that we have been enjoying each other."

My mouth dropped, *husband?* I waved her goodbye and drove off. I never saw her again, not even at work. Did she disappear? I do not know!"

"Ok," the Blind Man said. "Number three. Mild-Spice—Lucia, meaning 'light.'"

Monday night, we were sitting on the patio. Addie and Sherry brought glasses of wine in plastic cups, (no drinks in glass containers on the patio), salt-free crackers and three types of cheese. The table continued to gather a large number of people who discussed VOP and world problems. The noise level raised as everyone talked, *at the same time*, about their versions of gossip. People talked over one another. Three people spoke to each other, about three different subjects. How they understood each other, let alone answer each other's questions, is beyond me.

The Blind man sat silent. Frustrated, he started running his fingers across his piano keyboard to some unknown tunes. The more people talked, the louder he played.

Soon people quit talking. They began looking at each other then started to leave and return to their homes, I guess.

Eventually, Bob, Guillermo, and I were left sitting by ourselves. The wine, crackers, and cheese had been consumed by the departed.

Guillermo asked, "Did you understand any of that random talk?"

Bob said, "No, and now is a good time to tell us the story of your forth Spice Girl."

"Is that all you think about Bob, affairs with the girls in my life?"

"Since you put it that way, yes. Just two more 'Spice Girls' so we can set up a marketing program for you and the spice's you make so well and sell."

Guillermo started again, "Laura and I sat on the second step of her front porch. The full moon, big as a quarter, shined brightly in the sky. It seemed like the *man in the moon* was watching us.

Laura told me, 'you ready to fight is an example of life's survival and death. Roll the dice, *snake eyes*—you lose. *Seven*—you can search the night for sex, and the spice that goes with it.' She clasped my hand and raised it to her firm breast.

She kissed me hard and long. We got up and walked into her house. Inside stars filled the room like the fourth of July. The stars sprinkled down as the evening climaxed.

Hot coffee with sugar and cream added, we sat at the kitchen table until dawn. Laura gently hinted, "It is time you go big guy. Call me tomorrow when you get off work."

I put on my shoes and grabbed my coat, then kissed Laura good night or morning. "Ok, I will call tomorrow."

Our relation continued until she received a promotion and was reassigned to Santa Rosa, Ca. We maintained a long-distance relationship until the distance came between us.

Our love shattered, and life together shifted to love another.

The Big Man's eyes are tired. It seemed he was crying inside at the end of his memory.

After a long pause, Guillermo finally said, "Remember the Lyrics from the singing cowboy Gene Autry, 'You are my Sunshine?' The song is perfect for my feelings of Laura."

"My days turned black. I became mixed up, started to drink, go to the wrong parties, almost getting into serious trouble. Josh, a school friend, turned LAPD, was patrolling the streets in his police car. He saw me stumbling down the road, bumping into walls, trees, and vehicles. He stopped and sat me down on the curb. We had an old-fashion reunion in which I spilled my inner feelings.

Circumstance forced his hand, and Josh put me in the back seat of his squad car. His Christian side drove me to the church we went to as kids. He took me inside and turned me over to the priest. I sat in the last pew, the first row upon entering the church. Josh and the priest talked, I assume. I laid down on the church pew. I lost consciousness and fell asleep.

Time had passed, how much, I don't know. The priest walked me to the kitchen. There I had a cup of coffee and two tuna sandwiches. Josh walked in and slapped my back. 'Hello, *Big Guy*. It's been a long time; No see,' he said.

We had a long talk, which I appreciated. Then I thanked the priest for a meal and his guidance. I also thanked Josh for not giving me a ticket or taking me to jail. It was my *wake-up* call.

That experience turned a page in my life. I went to work harder than before. After work, I got my tamale cart out and ran the street till 10 PM. On weekends and holidays, I catered private parties, church functions, and car dealership celebrations, to mention a few.

Hot tamales were a great hit at the dealerships. With money in my pocket I eyed and bought a Dodge Van. It had pinstripes, big wheels in back and smaller wheels in front. Inside it was decked-out, ready to travel. It had a trailer hitch that fit the tamale cart as if it were custom made.

The next day with a Tamale cart in tow I wanted to show the priest the new set of wheels and sit the Tamale cart in his parking lot. Before I could get set up a police car arrived with its red lights flashing. A big boy's *Adam's apple* dropped to the bottom of his stomach. Then the flashing red lights went out. I looked closer and saw Josh in full uniform with a partner. "Any tamales buddy? Were hungry.'

The big lump cleared in the big man's throat then said, 'Yes, sir.'

While I was preparing tamales, the priest came out and talked with Josh and me. 'I am glad you both reunited. Guillermo, you 'Received the Lord'—his guidance led you back on a positive track. I am happy for you.' He then asked, "Do you have a tamale for this hungry priest." He finished by saying, "Bless you, boys. May the good Lord protect you, always?"

"Guillermo, the Tamale was good, thank you." The priest said.

"That is good," Bob and I agreed. "We will call Spice Girl number four, Laura... She may have moved on as you did, but Laura means *crowned with successes*—which she did, for your new beginning." "That sounds nice," Guillermo said.

Guillermo continued, "The following weeks after work I looked at where I had been! Not very glamorous!

One day I was sitting quietly in a chair I keep attached to my tamale cart, fastened behind my Dodge Van, drinking a cold soda and daydreaming.

The sun was warm. 'Hi! My name is Judy, and I heard your tamales are the best in town.'

I could not see her. The sun was directly in my eye's line of sight, causing a glow around her face. I shifted to the left; she moved right.

There, standing before me was a gorgeous, soft-haired, young lady. Uncontrollable I said, 'Wow! And yes! You came to the best cart, with the best Tamales in town.'

It was not long before Judy, and I begin traveling around town. We went to movies, malls, church, and car shows together. I believe it was instant love. I looked into her eyes, held her soft golden hair in my hand, and said, 'Judy, will you marry me?'

'Oh, Guillermo! I thought you would never ask,

Yes, I will marry you!'"

If there is anything better than to be loved it is loving [12]

Anonymous

"Now, Blind Man, and you Silver Fox, that was thirty-one plus years ago. Since then, we have raised a good, smart, happy girl—together. She works in Texas, at a Bio Teck Lab.

You know her as Judy, the white-haired lady who joins me for donuts on Friday, and the patio when she is not working.

Here is what I want you both to understand. The way to love is to realize that love might, at any moment, not survive and become lost. Go to bed happy, wake up happy, or alone."

Bob makes a declaration. "Judy becomes the fifth Spice Girl. You get no more spice from this life. Is that clear?"

"Yes, that is very clear. Judy is a perfect fifth Spice Girl. She is soft-haired and famous around the table under the umbrella— and a happy lady!" Guillermo gladly admits.

"I want to clarify a new marketing strategy. To sum up your spice from not hot to super-hot looks like this:

#1. Not-Hot-Spice Girl, **Sofia** – has its origins in Greek and means "wisdom."

#2. Warm-Spice Girl, **Maria** – Spanish version of Mary, which has many origins from—Italian meaning 'beautiful,' to Latin meaning 'ransom,' 'merciful,' and 'virgin.'

#3. Mild-Spice Girl, **Lucia** – Latin in origin, meaning 'light.'

#4. Hot-Spice Girl, **Laura** – in Spanish the name means 'crowned with successes.'

#5. Supper Hot-Spice Girl, **Judy** – French, Latin in origin meaning 'soft-haired' and 'youthful.' Characteristics: Communicative, Creative, Optimistic, Popular, Social, Dramatic, and Happy."

Guillermo continues to make customer request spices by the numbers. He is strictly word of mouth marketing and does not want to grow any more significant at this time. Bob and I disagree with Guile's marketing plan.

There is one thing we do agree on," Guillermo stated:

"There is only one true love in our life.
But a thousand and one copies."

Guillermo

The Dancers

Robert R. Torres

Bob-Cat dancing the night away

Chapter 10

Crazies

We are all a little crazy at some point in our lives.

I remember experimenting with speed on a hill named Hollywood Way near our Newport Beach home. My brother, six years old and I seven, took our Red Flyer Wagon to the hilltop. We planned to ride our Red Flyer down the steep hill as fast as it would go.

Ready, we started slowly—picked up speed going fast—then faster—then the steering handle began to shimmy in my hand. I could no longer control the Red Flyer. I could not slow it down as it went even faster. The wheels turned—the steering handle jerked out of my hand. Then the high-speed crash. We fell to the asphalt and tumbled to a stop. Our skin was torn and scraped, leaving skin patches on the pavement. We were a bloody mess and crying.

The challenging part of our venture was going home and explaining our injury to mother. Mom had the wickedest remedy, worst then the asphalt rash. Using the bottle of 1945 alcohol, she poured it into our wounds to get the little rocks out. Truthfully, the small stones felt like boulders and the alcohol like fire.

Her reprimand, "You boys, do not do that again. Now go feed your pigeons and Billy," she ordered.

Billy was our friend, a playful goat that butts us with his horns. He pulled our Red Flyer Wagon and mowed the yard. Billy kept the grass cut short because dad was not always available. Dad was a fireman who worked at El Toro Marine Corps Air Base, located in Irvine, California, now-closed. In his off time from being a fireman, he would fish one of the three commercial fishing boats he owned.

Dad's boat, "Bonnie Breeze," was named for our mother. I rode in the crow's nest when I was only three months old. I do not remember the trip. I did see pictures with my mother holding me.

Now back to Billy and being free from that burning alcohol! My brother and I ran as fast as possible out the back door into the backyard. Outside I tripped on my bib-overalls falling face-first to the ground, again. I dirtied my clean clothes pant leg, now stained green with grass on the knee. My hands hurt, now filled with fresh dirt. It was not my day.

The second time I felt the need for speed, I was fifteen and just purchased a used Cushman motor scooter. I could deliver newspapers faster than before and still get to school on time. One day, traveling a two-lane boulevard as quick as the motor scooter would go, I ran a stop sign. Running the stop sign was the easy part. The tough part was running the stop sign in front of a policeman sitting in his squad car. I think, *"He was waiting for me?"*

He did not give me a ticket. He told me to drive home, slowly, and park the scooter—and tell my father how and that I ran the stop sign. He also advised that I go to the DMV to get a learner driving permit.

For those seniors who forgot what DMV is necessary—but dreaded—Department of Motor Vehicle who giveth and taketh away our state-regulated driving license.

The next day the policeman came to the house to see if I had discussed my speeding problem with my father, which I had. The policeman brought a driver's test booklet and suggested *I read it.* I was allowed to drive the scooter to deliver newspapers ONLY until I received a learner's permit or driver's license.

I dread to think what would have happened if I pulled that type of a stunt today? A ticket, a crash, maybe a death or something worse?

I am sure you are thinking of that one crazy thing you did in your life a long time ago or more recently. I would love to hear your story and print it. Right now, share your story with someone. Remember it is okay to exchange your crazy, silly stories with someone. Try to get them to smile, or better—to laugh. I bet they will tell you their embarrassing tales in return.

From there to here, and here to there,
Funny things are everywhere. [13]

Here at VOP, we have Ron (Roddy) and Bobcat (Karen), husband and wife. They are a beautiful couple with some issues like the rest of us. Ron is a retired roofer who fell many years ago and injured his back. Twenty-five years later, Ron is driving his automobile, stopped at a red light. While sitting at the red light, a drunk driver hit him. His back was injured again and the car destroyed.

Police reports, insurance, and court issues all blamed the roofer, not the other driver. Poor Ron!

Two years later, he is still working on the case. Good luck, Ron.

Ron and Bobcat are right and good for each other. Ron is happy, upbeat, but does not walk well. On karaoke night in the clubhouse, Ron and Bobcat tap their canes to the beat of the music.

At least once during the evening they will get up and dance to a 50's rock and rolling tune. They dance holding on to each other, bobbing their heads to the rhythm of a song.

Ron and Bob, the Blind Man, continued talking when Ron said, "Life is a Gift! Today before we think of saying an unkind word think of someone who cannot speak, hear, or see."

"Are you talking about me, Ron?" the Blind Man asked.

"No Bob, you see through your imagination, the wisdom of blindness and musical humor. Think of the blind person who was born blind. That is blind!"

Interrupting, "What is everyone doing?" Albie asked.

"Can't you see we are drinking wine, eating crackers, counting how many donuts each person is taking and who drinks regular or decaf coffee? Oh! Yes, we count coupons too."

"Can you share some wine?" Albie asked. Without taking a breath, he stated, "I do not see any coupons, and no one is eating donuts."

Puzzled, Albie uttered, "Tuesday! Today is Tuesday, not Friday. Aren't donuts on Friday? Come on, guys. Are you kidding? Are you not?"

"Oh! You are right. Must we have been doing something else? By the way, do you like it here, Albie? Are you going to stay or take your lovely wife and return to New York?" I asked with a hint of sarcasm.

"No, the children are here. My wife will not let them go."

"Albie, it looks like you tried to cut your hair yourself, then forgot to comb it. If you need a barber, ask. I cut hair on the battlefields of Vietnam for a week; I will be glad to help."

No comment came from Albie.

Then Albie said, "Did you hear about the mom and her crazy?"

I replied, "Stop, stop right there before you start pointing the finger or condemning someone. Remember not one of us, including you, is without sin. We all answer to one Maker! Be careful talking about others."

I continued, "Remember, if you have depressing thoughts that seem to get you down, stop, put a sock in it, or best put a smile on your face. Thank your wife for feeding you. Then thank God you are still around, alive, and walking. Life is a gift. We need to *Live, Enjoy, and Celebrate* to *fulfill life* Albie. Please sit down. Did you understand those word of wisdom?" I asked.

Ron the roofer, Bob the Blind Man, Guillermo the Refrigerator, and Dave, the guitarist, all clapped with joy and said, "Way to go Silver Fox!"

Sam, quivering in his seat, hurriedly asked Albie, "What happened with, you know, the Bingo Cop, Mrs. Sumo, and her daughter?"

Albie did not answer Sam's question.

Joseph quickly spoke up. "She is getting kicked out by order of the management because her thirty-five-year-old daughter continues to cause trouble. This time the daughter, who is not even old enough to be here, accused their neighbor Michael, a retired store manager, of inappropriate advances. *He is not even here.* He is in Pasurobles, California, surfing and staying at his daughter's house for over two weeks. He will return to sad news next week on Saturday."

Susan, a pleasant-looking 76-year-old lady with a soft commanding voice, had enough of the discriminating talk. She spoke out, "Before you boys continue talking about someone's dirty house that they did not clean or sweep properly, think about the people who are living in the streets. With minimal shelter, eating minimal food, begging, and unable to get to the local shelter or a doctor. Think? It could be anyone of you. So knock it off." She then continued opening her evening's junk mail.

She continued, with beautiful eyes and an attractive smile, said, "Smile, and let me tell you about the Casino Night that none of you showed up. The food was good, compliments of the management. They served sliced ham, mashed potatoes, vegetables, with a drink and dessert. Everyone enjoyed playing roulette and singing. We had a good time. I know that the two of you, Silver Fox and Addie, had medical problems, but why did you three not go?"

Sam said, "I heard Mrs. Thailand's African Gray bird sing, '*What's Love Got to do with it*' and asked, '*Where is Gary* and *Hit the Road, Jack?*'

We did not have to go inside and listen to him sing. CC entertained us out here."

I was relieved, but the others at the table had no excuse. *Sorry guys,* I thought.

Mary said, "This place is sometimes nuts, and it starts here with this table."

Bob, the Blind Man, followed up saying, "I cannot see but what I hear is not only crazy, it is as Mary said, *it is Nuts.* It starts not out here but behind those glass windows and doors."

006.5 quietly interjected, "It is like the little guy with the goatee and tattoos. He runs around insulting someone for no reason. He sneaks back to apologize and tells the offended he was only kidding. It makes people upset, although most people understand him. I cannot remember his name. You know who I mean."

We cannot forget dear Mildred (81) who is called the traffic/parking enforcer. She is 4'-7", 140 pounds — a beautifully controlled kick-ass person who never married. She lives alone and still drives. VOP has no assigned parking for it's residents. If you have a doctor excuse, or letter, with an explanation to management, they may or may not assign you a personal-reserved parking spot. About ninety percent of the parking spots are handicapped reserved. Mildred, who has never been sick, watches for people who park incorrectly.

She then reports them to management.

She has a backup plan—a foul mouth, full of profanity who believes he can rearrange the parking system and make everyone happy. It will be hard because there are 220 apartments and only 200 spots, not counting the visitors or handicap required spots. Good luck to anyone who wants to fix the parking difficulties.

Every day Mildred goes out for lunch then doggie-bags dinner home. She does not leave tips because she believes people should work for a wage. Therefore it is not necessary to give a restaurant server a service tip. She often told people, "No one ever gave me a tip for working."

When Mildred returns home and cannot find a place to park, she looks for a parking violator and reports them or calls a tow truck to have the vehicle removed. Management one day made an exception to their parking rule and gave Mildred a parking spot. Since then, no one has been towed or reported. Now you can set your watch to her daily lunchtime departure and return.

Is Mildred crazy? No, I do not think so? I do believe she is a little strange, but aren't we all?

Dogs, known as man's best friend, are excellent companions for many seniors. The VOP canines range from little, small, medium, and large. Man's best friends are cute, yes! And some are not so. There are short, medium, and long-haired dogs; with and without spots. Some residents must have two dogs so their pets can have a friend.

Are there rules for dogs? Oh yes! It starts with a large dollar deposit and picture: a mugshot with a reward amount. Fido's recorded in the lease agreement with a censorship footnote: **No Barking**. Excessive barkers are subject to owners' eviction. Residents should not walk their dogs in the common property area, clubhouse, or swimming pool patio area, and all dogs must be on a six-foot leash at all time.

As I write at this very time, on the inside walkway of building 'C', a small white mutt on a twelve-foot leash pulls it's master as fast as she can walk. The senior, a beautiful redhead, is wearing a long formal blue evening gown. Stylishly dressed, she also wears a blue plastic glove on her right hand and a rhinestone bracelet on her left wrist. She is attached to her pooch. Daily, she wears a different colored formal long dress that drags behind her, sweeping the walkway.

Different dogs meet nightly, about five p.m., on the walkway by the big trees. The meeting is always after the office closes, and management goes home.

At the same time, an overweight straggle-haired lady walks her oversized lapdog down the inside walkway of 'B' building. She stops her dog from letting it smell the plants and scratch the dirt outside my window to do its business. After a reasonably qualified deposit, she must bend over and pick up Fido's poop with her beautiful blue plastic glove. When someone is watching, she remembers her *lease contract* of picking up her dog's mess. Sometimes she forgets to pick up Fido's toilet. That is when she thinks no one is watching her.

I think bending over is a strain on her waistline.

There is more after the dog has a good poop. The straggly haired lady intersects with the long formal dressed redhead. Here the two dogs begin their nightly yapping and tug of war. I think the dogs start barking to protect their masters. The barking and yapping last about two minutes. The redhead and her fluffy white pooch must have won the dogs' argument because they go towards the double glass doors and elevator.

The overweight lady and her dog turn right, then left, to disappear around the corner.

All dogs are not dangerous, sick, or evil. Some are very polite. The example: Violet, a white—medium-sized York. She gets appropriately escorted to the dog park. Along the way, she entertains residents. Violet, when walking, will rear on her hind legs and walk like people. I do not believe she barks. When someone stops to talk Violet will sit quietly and raise her right paw while waiting for a handshake.

Then there is Charlie, a beautiful shorthaired brown Dachshund. Charlie's owner is a sixty-eight-year-old lovely lady who walks her baby maybe five times a day. Charlie is so polite he will lay down and wait for his leading lady to exchange puppy talk. He always barks "Hello" at me. He responds to, "Hey Charlie. Roll over. Sit. Shake hands," commands without hesitation.

There is this ninety-year-old woman with a very small Chihuahua named Kong. She walks, or rides Kong using a small child's baby carriage, treating her like a baby.

There are many respectable owners with good dog stories, and some not so good. Let us not get into those stories at this time.

The cute, medium-sized, long-haired black dog followed by a tall, slim, black-haired owner stops at Mrs. Thailand's garden patio. The dog, Mertal, stays, and talks with Mrs. Thailand's caged bird when on the patio. The African Gray with a red tail is named Choke Chi meaning *Victory*. He was hand-fed from a six-week-old chick cared for by his mother, Mrs. Thailand. He is now a talkative twenty-six-year-old.

Mertal brings, or sometimes drags, her master, stopping to bark a sweet yap getting Choke Chi's, CC's attention. CC, will return a dogs bark telling Mertal, "Hello." Mertal replies with "Bark, Bark." CC often sings Mertal a song from Tina Turner's 1984 collection, *"What's Love got to do with it."*

Choke Chi's version singing to Mertal is *"Love to do with it."*

On other occasions, CC will advise Mertal and strangers to "go take a bath," which everyone thinks is hilarious. CC tells Thomas and his dog "goodbye" every time they stop. Yes, CC is temperamental and will talk to some and not others. He sings and speaks the most when we are away, people tell us.

You may wonder how many dogs live here in this beautiful complex. Every morning while sitting at my computer, sipping decaf coffee, I count six dogs walking their owners toward the dog park. How many more dogs there are, I do not know.

Many mornings I count four to six fluffy-tailed squirrels playing in the tree. With them are three large black birds that forage for food the squirrels hide around the trees. The blackbirds remind me of the "Men in Black," the movie with, ah! You know, those two guys. Oh yes! Tommy Lee Jones and Will Smith.

How about the crazy Blind Man? He has a pair of dogs measuring about fourteen inches, they are unofficially named *Left,* and *Right* by the residents of VOP since he never named them. They are very obedient. They know on command when to get up and go. Every day Bob grabs the dog leashes to take them for a walk. He holds tight so as not to lose the strap. His dogs are well-trained and follow along, never causing anyone problems. They never bark, even at our bird Choke Chi.

It is terrific how the blind man takes his dogs everywhere: to the mailroom, grocery store, doctor's office, and the patio where they sit under an umbrella. With supervision, the Blind Man will take his dogs into the swimming pool. They play well together. Management overlooks Bob and his dogs.

The other day Bob, Claud, Guillermo and I went for a two and one half-mile walk. No time limits, just exercise. When we returned home, Bob said, "I have to go upstairs and rest my dogs." Upstairs he placed his dogs' leash, cane, on a wall hook. He filled a big pan with water for his tired dogs.

After a good soaking and a power nap, the Blind Man put on his size fourteen shoes. He grabbed his blind man's stick and sauntered down to the patio under the umbrella. He joined the gals and guys discussing world problems and the latest gossip.

Properly trained, man can be dog's best friend.

[14] Corey Ford,

Let us switch this man/dog thing around and think from a dog's point of view. This is a cute story rewritten from a story? (2018) by William Tozzi, *"What Does He Want From Me Now"* [14.2].

Here he comes! What does he want from me this time? Oh! He has a leash in his hand. That means it is time to walk him. Oh goody!

Let us see, he likes me to wag my tail, and run in circles; he thinks it is fun? I will let him grab my collar to hook the leash. I tug him to the front door. Outside he wants to go right, and I want to go left. I pull the rope harder, so we go left. He lets me stop at the yellow fire hydrant for my first pit stop. Boy, do I have him trained?

Down the street, I notice there is canine activity. I see the cute little bitch. The female canine has a fancy diamond-studded collar and a pink bow. She is walking towards me so I will wag my tail to get her attention. What happened? Why did she ignore me?

The next time we see each other, she will notice me, maybe?

I continue to drag my master down the path. Goody, I's that time. I see the lush garden with the sign: **Keep Off**. I will sniff the ground for my marked territory under the tree. Is it the tree the Silver Fox claims is his? I will rotate in circles, squat, and deposit my poop. Then, I will scratch the ground with my hind legs, indicating: finished. It is called "flushing the toilet." If he wants, my master will pick up my droppings in the little blue bag he gets to carry until we get home.

Poor guy.

At home, he opens my bag of treats. Why doesn't he give them to me? No, he makes me sit, shake hands and roll-over before I get a doggie treat. When he runs out of my favorite treat, I stop doing my tricks and return to my favorite napping spot under his computer table. I will nap until he wants to take an additional afternoon walk.

If dogs could talk, perhaps we'd find it just as hard
to get along with them as we do people. [14.1]

Karel Capek 1890-1938 journalist

A dog named 'Two Legs' watches "Days of our Lives." She begs her owner to turn on the television every day at 1:00 p.m. When meeting and greeting people or showing off to other canines, she stands upright on her hind legs. I guess she wants to be a person?

There are many more residents with cute dogs — some who observe their lease law and those that do not.

Every first Tuesday of the month, our residence council hears complaints about dogs and parking I mentioned earlier. Month to month, things change—the good to sad—and back again.

Move, you say? No, I like my tree outside my window, the swimming pool and free coffee when it is available. This complex of two-hundred or more units has its share of crazies. Many walk the pathways with their pet. We smile, stop, and discuss the latest medical problems, weather and who moved out—speculating why.

For the crazies, when the 9:00 PM evening news is over its past their bedtime. They join the ranks of the tired and fall asleep. By 2:00 AM they get the late-night urge to *pee*. Finished, they cannot go back to sleep. They lay on the bed, counting sheep, watch television, or dream up new medical troubles.

We do not have seniors living bazaar (market) lives here at VOP. What we have is the bizarre (kooky) type. I said it; that *must* mean Me, Bob and Guillermo. My first winter at VOP in the clubhouse I have a very bizarre story to tell. I will call it "Cold Feet."

It was Tuesday, Bingo Day for the semi-living in the recreation room and clubhouse. I was at the community mailboxes where Bill and I greeted each other. We wondered how many trees had been cut to deliver the advertisements we received in the day's mail. We may have looked at them; I do not remember. What we did do with our junk mail was file them into the recycle bin along with everyone else.

 On this cold winter morning, I zipped my coat up high. It was cold, overcast and gloomy, with a slight drizzle of rain outside.

"Goodbye Bill, see you next time,"

Bill acknowledged and said, "Ok."

In the recreation area, twenty die-hard Bingo players were standing, crowded together at the clubhouse double glass door and windows, viewing out into the patio and swimming pool area. A strange, curious, feeling of the *bizarre* entered my mind.

I asked Jane, an 82-year-old retired school teacher, "What is so interesting?"

Deana and Jim both turned and said, "You will never believe what is on the patio! A bear! Come look for yourself."

"What! A bear?" I said with a choked-up voice.

Wedging myself between the onlookers, I was startled to see what everyone saw.

Sitting in the patio, in a white patio chair, under a folded down umbrella is a white polar bear the size of a man. Its white furry back poised for all the clubhouse onlookers to see, or was it?

Herb, an ancient relic of a resident, said, "I will call nine-one-one." Then asked, "Does anyone know the telephone number of nine-one-one?"

No one answered Herb. John standing next to Herb, said, "Press the emergency button on your phone.

He did. A voice answers, "Nine-eleven, what is your emergency?"

Herb said, "There is a bear on the patio, and I need the phone number for nine-one-one."

Dispatcher: "This is nine-one-one."

Herbs, confused, "You said this was nine-eleven."

The dispatcher, "Sir, nine-one-one, and nine-eleven are the same."

Herb nervous, excited and concerned about the white bear on the patio, told the dispatcher, "I may be old, but I am not stupid. Nine-One-One and Nine-Eleven are not the same number," and hung up the phone.

I stepped outside to get a closer look at the Polar Bear. I was shocked, puzzled, and surprised? A Polar Bear on the patio, under a folded down umbrella with red shoes. A closer look reveals it was Albie—the New York-retired employment-headhunter. We know as the *Do you like it here,* guy.

"You old fool! What are you doing dressed like a polar bear sitting next to a cold water swimming pool? Do you know that you have those people scared of a Polar Bear on the patio?

He looked at me and smiled, "I am waiting for 11:11 AM. That is the time I will jump into the pool and participate in this year's Polar Bear swim marathon."

Great, I looked at the clubhouse double glass door with people's noses pressed against the glass and puzzled looks on their faces. I waved at the curious and said, "It is ok. It's not a white polar bear, its Albie, the bizarre being kooky."

My head regularly shakes-rattles and rolls with mysteries and disbelief here at VOP. I continually tell myself, I *will get through these bewildering days and that VOP, is a Very Odd Place.* I often wonder—*what will tomorrow bring?* Writing this book *The Blind Man, Big Man and Silver Fox.*

"Boy, you are a strange duck, *quack-quack,* "You know the pool is *not* heated but super cold at this time of the year. Look, the bubbles from the filters are coming out—*frozen.*"

"You are kidding," he said. "They are not frozen. It is cold air."

Shaking my head side to side, "You remember that you do not swim during the warm summer month when the water is warm?" "I know. You are right, and I am cold already."

I looked at the clubhouse glass window—the people continued looking out with puzzled faces. I waved at the curious once again and said, "It is ok. Go play Bingo. It is not a white bear, its Albie, the *bizarre* being *kooky*."

The window cleared rapidly with everyone returning to their Bingo cards.

Albie looked at me, cold and shivering, he said, "I believe I should go home and get a cup of coffee and rethink this Polar Bear thing."

"Home, Yes! You should. Just do not go into the clubhouse dressed like your artificial-imitation Polar Bear self."

I shook my head, went into the clubhouse, and said, "Just kooky Albie."

Someone shouted, "Let us play BINGO!"

I poured myself a cup of decaf coffee. I looked around the room to see the bingo players in deep concentration. I thought to myself *go home with my junk mail and the military-grade coffee and relax.*

Chapter 11

Tomorrow

Sometimes life seems unpleasant, unreasonable, ugly, and not fair. When you feel this way, remember life always offers you a second chance. A second chance is called *tomorrow.*

With the new day comes new strength

And new thoughts. [15]

Eleanor Roosevelt

I hope this humor and these absurdities make you laugh. These stories, embellished—hopefully—do not offend, upset, or insult anyone. It helps if you have a sense of humor to get through the day and into tomorrow. Tomorrow always brings new adventures.

Today, before someone complains about life, *reach out to someone,* and make them laugh. Share a conversation with someone to bring a smile, hopefully—and some laughter. Humor can open an unlimited number of doors to better yourself and help others.

Albie reminded us, *"Tomorrow, Tomorrow,"* then tried to remember the lyrics.

The Blind Man tapped his keyboard to the beat of Alicia Morton's *Tomorrow.*

Guille searched his cell phone for 'tomorrow.' He found Willie Nelson, 1973—*Three Days, Yesterday, Today, and Tomorrow.* I liked it as a song but not for this section of the book. Who wants three days of hate, tears, and sorrow?

Yesterday is over, let us forget about it. Today we want to interact with others—happily. Find happy feelings to help rid your medical or other problems. Tonight, before bed, pray for a good day tomorrow.

Guillermo continued to search for versions of *Tomorrow* on his cell phone.

I tapped *Tomorrow* on the table with a pair of drumsticks, not chicken legs.

The Blind man said, "Not bad Silver Fox, you have the rhythm."

Albie said, "Silver Fox, you had better not quit your day job!"

Guillermo blurted out, not taking his eyes off his cell-phone, "Gary, you would like *'Yesterday When I Was Young,'* by Roy Clark—1996."

Everyone repeated, "Yes, terror day? No way, not 'Yesterday' because it is 'Today' and will soon be 'Tomorrow.'"

Guillermo, in his deep cold voice, tried to sing, *"Da da, da, da . . ."*

"Guille! No." I cut him off before he could sing the chorus. "Here at VOP, most residents are already old; they or their loved ones are not spring chickens and do not need reminding. Their divorce was most likely destructive, and they want to forget. They also do not need to be reminded of their lonely heart."

The table agreed.

"Guillermo, the song, *'Yesterday, When I Was Young'* —maybe that is for you and your feelings. I feel you need to see your psychiatrist first thing 'Tomorrow.' Maybe first you should, please, stop at your séance, tort or palm reader for an update. Or, see your Hindu, swami, ascetic yogis who can kindle and bring you into today's happy rhythms we like to hear under the umbrella.

Besides, I like 'Tomorrow,' let us stick with that."

Albie again chimed in, in his unusual and discharging way, singing the two-worded tune, *'Tomorrow, Tomorrow.* Alicia Morton lyrics "Tomorrow" by Annie is a beautiful song from the Broadway Musical, "Annie." *The sun will come out tomorrow, bet your bottom dollar….*

I continued, "Guile, see? Even Albie understands we need a bright and sunny day. Sun brings brightness into hearts. Today may be glum, like Annie, but the sun will come out tomorrow.

Annie is a story that follows a mischievous (senior) Orphan Annie in her quest to locate her parents (freedom and peace of mind). Along the way, she learns what it means to trust someone, but most importantly, she learned how to love—especially herself.

A slight change to Annie's story allows it to reflect VOP and its seniors that inhabit its compound:

VOP is a story that follows mischievous, naughty, playful fifty-five-year-old, and older senior's quests to locate their golden year dreams. Along the way, they learn what it means to age, be gossiped about, whom to trust and who not to trust. How to enjoy living alone and how to get to the doctor if they no longer drive.

Seniors worry and hope their caretakers will not abuse or take advantage of them.

Some learn how to love themselves and to say, "Can I help you?"

Another senior wanders into the swimming pool area to sit under the patio's umbrella. The pack of jackals, already sitting outside, talking; they accept that life is not a fairy tale, and sometimes it sucks. The jackals console the squawking whiners and joke with old foxes as they look to pass the time. Soon a smile emerges, and they go home happy.

One day an elderly lady came onto the patio, something she avoids because she is afraid she may fall into the swimming pool. She was looking for help on how to connect her new telephone for the hard of hearing. George went to help her solve the minor problem she described. Now we are affectionately known as the *public service table.*

George could not fix the telephone, so he called her service company. They came right away and adequately attached her phone. It now works for her the way she likes it.

Think of us this way—a table of jackals, not the bushy-tailed, long-legged canines with large ears. We are three guys, some dolls, who confide to confuse and perform non-routine simple tasks for one-another in need. We often agree life sucks—if that is what you want to hear.

If you walk around in the clubhouse or outside in the pool area with one shoe on and one red sock, we will agree you are strange. If it's late, we will agree with each other and tell you that *you're stoned, drunk, intoxicated, tanked, or plastered.* We even let you pick your favorite word for drunkenness. Then our advice: *stop drinking, go home, and sleep it off. Come back tomorrow when sober and clear-headed and tell us all about your fun.*

We hear daily: *"Tomorrow I have to go to the doctor." "My back hurts,"* or some other part of the body. *"Tomorrow I have to go for cataract surgery."* Or maybe, *"Oliver is going in tomorrow, or Wednesday, for knee replacement at 6:00 AM."*

We do not hear: *"Tomorrow Millie is coming over from the senior center to show us how to do needlework."* Or, *"Chang - is coming over to demonstrate how to perform chi the proper way."* I have never heard anyone say they *"have to change the oil in the car tomorrow."* Nothing along those lines.

So today is here. Do we wait for tomorrow, doing nothing today? No. You can always exercise your body by walking briskly around the apartment complex a couple of times today.

Three ladies were sitting in the clubhouse eating donuts reminiscing. One lady stopped me and said, "I saw you exercising this morning. That is good; keep it up; it is good."

I answered, "Thank you. Yes, it is good. I like to do some form of exercise every day and go to the gym two times a week."

The second lady said, "That is good."

"Thank you, ladies; I will be glad to walk with you if you want." I was turned down with each having a different excuse. I then asked, "How about tomorrow?" Dead Silence.

The three Jackals sat by themselves. I switched the conversation towards the Blind Man.

We learned earlier Bob was born in East Los Angeles, Boyle Heights, in 1945.

Bob joined the United States Marine Corp. He became sick, requiring him to enjoy Boot Camp, *twice*. His military job training: Court Reporting. After the military, he continued court reporting in the Los Angeles court system. He formed his own company employing thirty people. Slowly becoming blind, he ultimately lost his company to a greedy family member.

Today, Bob lives in a senior apartment complex. He intermingles with the guys and gals on the patio under an umbrella in Santa Clarita, California. As the Silver Fox, I cunningly asked the blind man, "What were the most famous court cases you recorded.

In the military or the civil court?"

After meddling, prodding, and questioning, Bob finally answered. "Military."

Marines continually returned home from the war zones of Vietnam to Camp Pendleton, Oceanside, California. Here they relocated to new duty stations. Some were retrained and received new duty assignments. Other marines needed various medical treatments or mental needs.

In 1969 the commander of the *Military Court of Justice* called Sergeant Robert S. (Bob) to his office. The commander, a military judge, three other officers, and Sergeant Robert S. were assigned to preside over a murder trial. Sergeant Robert S. chosen for his "A" rated accuracy for trial-script recording.

The Case of the Drunk Murder

"During re-training two marines, PFC Gilmer and PFC Cramer received weekend passes. They rode a military bus from Camp

Pendleton to a San Diego drop-off point. They signed into a hotel reserved for GIs. The two wandered the San Diego beach streets, skirt-chasing, shopping, and drinking.

It was late, Gilmer talked wildly—bragging and boasting, being disproportionately proud about achievements during this recent tour in Vietnam. Gilmer bragged about a specific, and traumatic, firefight in which he had participated.

While on patrol in a Kong-infested area Gilmer's squad was surprised with a horrific ground attack. Many Marines died or were injured while others ran to safety. Gilmer stepped into the jungle brush. Standing his ground, he returned AR-16 fire, killing many of the enemies.

A Staff Sergeant listening came to Gilmer and stated, '*Cool it* and soften the firefight description.'

Gilmer jumped up and told the sergeant, "F*** off. You were not there; *I was.*"

Cramer jumped between the two marines and told Gilmer, '*Chill out,*' trying to calm down his outrage.

The Staff Sergeant then said, 'You boys have had enough to drink and better go sleep it off.'

Both men said, 'OK.' They peacefully left the bar. For where?

Outside Gilmer hailed a Yellow Cab that stopped and negotiated a drop-off point. The men headed back toward the hotel where they were registered.

Gilmer and Cramer argued: *who is going to pay the cab fare?* Cramer thought the cab fare was costly. In his drunken state, he knew he could not walk the three-mile distance.

Gilmer placed his hands, covering his ears. He closed his eyes then started shaking all over. Was he upset at Cramer's question? Or was drunkenness causing his head to relive the Vietnam killings?

Cramer asked Gilmer, 'Are you ok? You look strange and not yourself.'

Yeah! I am ok. We better go. Do not worry; I will take care of the cab fare.'

Rambling, Cramer said, 'That will be just fine,' and jumped into the cab. He closed his eyes. In and out of sleep, he lay to the right of Gilmer with his head pressed against the window of the cab.

Gilmer, sitting behind the small-statured Mexican taxi driver, continued to shake. He feels confused—somewhere between alcohol and death. 'Driver, please pull to the side of the road next to that large, empty, weedy field.'

'Sure boss.' The driver rolled to a complete stop, leaving the taxi's engine running. He waited for instruction: where and what to do next? The cabbie admired a clear star-studded night sky. The *heavens are beautiful,* he thought.

Gilmer's Post-Traumatic Stress Disorder (PTSD) [16] reactivated from alcohol. He removed a large U.S. Marine corps Vietnam M7 Bayonet, commonly called a combat knife, from his waistband.

Cramer woke enough to ask, 'Are we at the hotel? I feel sick!'

'Sleep, I am going to take care of the taxi fare. I will wake you.'

Firmly gripping the military combat knife in his right hand, Gilmer slowly moved his weighted body closer to the driver's back. Swiftly he placed his left hand tightly over the taxi driver's mouth— forcing the man's head backward. Like a human-machine, his right hand squeezed tightly, the serrated combat knife raising above his head. With all his force, his body lunged forward. The knife's eight-inch blade repeatedly plunged into the driver's chest —slicing through the driver's shirt, skin, breastbone, cutting his ribs and puncturing his lung. The force is so hard the blade passed through the driver's chest, its tip exiting the drivers back, cutting into the driver's seat cushion.

Cramer heard a loud, muffled scream. He woke to listen to the commotion. Startled, Cramer saw a knife in Gilmer's hand and shouted, 'Gilmer, what did you just do?!'

Both men jumped out of the taxi and ran into the open field, away from the crime scene. The area happened to be behind the hotel they had rented a room in earlier.

The Cabbie did not die without a fight. With a military knife stuck in his chest, the cab driver exited his taxi and ran toward the pair standing in the field. The combat veterans watched the man fall to the ground at their feet.

The men returned to the hotel and slept the night away. In the morning they caught the bus back to Camp Pendleton. They joined their work assignments as usual.

The San Diego Police Department found the missing Yellow Cab with its engine running. The taxi driver is located, facedown, Dead in the nearby field.

Seven months after the event Cramer was inebriated and discussed with others the unsolved taxi murder. The bartender called 911, and the San Diego Police arrested the marine. They turned him and the case over to the Camp Pendleton military authorities.

Cramer is fully cooperating and explains how he witnessed Gilmer plunge the military-issued combat knife into the taxi driver's chest. Why? The Cabbie was charging too much for the three-mile fare. Scared and drunk, Cramer and Gilmer left the scene returning to Camp Pendleton.

The military court found both men guilty and immediately dishonorably discharged them boyh.

Cramer, who cooperated, was charged with accessory to the fact and was sentenced to ten years in a military prison. Gilmer, with PTSD, received 1st-degree murder charges—with circumstances. He received life in prison without the possibility of parole."

****

Bob finished his story in an enthused action with his body shaking all over. With his memory well jogged, he started again.

"Civil, one civil case? Let me think.

There were many civil cases with famous or well-known people — many well and unknown persons with millions needed depositions. There were many properties, land grant, and title disputes: divorce cases, auto accidents with wrongful death, and many more. If a person feels wronged, even in the slightest manner, there is a family that will argue against making a buck. Hollywood's divorces, film productions, music labels, and private business create numerous problems for civil litigation."

The Million Dollar Sucker Punch

"During a 1977 Los Angeles Lakers' and Huston Rockets' game at the Forum in Los Angeles, a fight between players erupted. With tempers flying Rudy Tomjanovich jumped from the Rockets bench startling Kermit Washington. The downward force of Tomjanovich speeding body slammed into Washington's fast-flying fist so hard it caused Tomjanovich multiple skull fractures. Injuries included: a broken nose, cracked eye socket, a severely torn tear duct, and other facial injuries.

My company was hired to obtain depositions from the players on both teams, that included management, coaches, and spectators that witnessed the punching. It took some time to deliver the many statements to the courts.

Tomjanovich recovered from his injuries and returned to playing basketball. He received an undisclosed award of approximately 1.8 million dollars. He became an NBA coach from 1983-2005. His last coaching assignment was with the Los Angeles Lakers 2004-2005 is now retired.

Washington, was expelled 26 games for the 1977 punch. His career managed to continue from 1973-1982. A Government investigation found that Washington's fundraising foundation funneled money from medical services for African kids with HIV to his personal needs. In 2004 Washington pleaded guilty to Tax Fraud and Identity Theft. At 66 years old Washington was sentenced to six years in federal prison by District Judge Greg Kays."

"Thanks, Bob, those were two fascinating and sad stories. I think I will go home and watch The Simpson's or a cartoon to cheer myself up. I have to put something happy into my head."

Guillermo asked, "Are you going to the BBQ tomorrow?"

"I'm not sure. Mrs. Thailand and I have an appointment in the valley. We plan to be home around five or so. We may eat out."

Guillermo, the refrigerator, and Bob, the Blind Man, both acknowledged the day and said, "Good Night."

"See you tomorrow, here under the umbrella," Bob whispered.

Whoever Gossips to You?

Will gossip about You.

Spanish Proverb

Chapter 12

Fallacy

Everyone is sitting around the patio telling stories they witnessed, were part of, read, or watched at the movies or on television. Some stories seem strange, others outstanding, with too many to print.

Life is like the ocean; it goes up and down.
It can be calm or still, rough or rigid but in the end,
It is always beautiful. [17]

It was a little after 6:00 PM. Mrs. Thailand and I were cooking a Tri-Tip roast on the BBQ listening to others tell their stories.

Albie, being his disillusioned self, made an off-color, unacceptable, and rude comment about women. Mrs. Thailand advised him to go home and to not talk like that again. She reminded residents to be careful, lock their doors, and be suspicious of strangers. Also, be sure you call 911—but not like Mrs. Applecrumby, the 91-year-old living in building 'D'.

It was around 2:30 PM, after Halloween and before Thanksgiving. No? It was the Thursday before Thanksgiving. The weather was getting cooler when all of a sudden everyone at VOP saw and heard a police helicopter circling above. Emergency vehicle sirens were screaming in the distance. Out of nowhere the driveway of VOP became jammed with police cars, an ambulance, fire trucks and even a black van that said SWAT.

There were more emergency vehicles in the compound then the recent "slip and fall" of Mr. Burt.

Police with loudspeakers warned, advised, and told residents to stay inside their apartments and to lock all doors. The cadre of police secured and guarded the entrance to the building. Uniformed officers interviewed everyone, including myself, asking if we had seen any suspicious persons lurking around.

About 4:00 PM, all the emergency vehicles disappeared except for one old car parked in the middle of the street. What happened?

Soon the news was spreading out of control with everyone having his or her particular version.

These are the words of Mrs. Applecrumby to the gathering of curious at a table on 'Donut Friday.'

The Missing Black Diamond

Detective Dang arrived in his old something green or blue faded, rusted, torn brown upholstery, 1954 Studebaker with a month's worth of fast-food wrappers inside. He parked his relic vehicle in the middle of the street. He wore a T-shirt that said: *No Bad Days*. He dangled a Beretta handgun slung in its shoulder holster, exposed.

He showed his detective badge to the officer standing at the door. He walked in and was greeted with, "I am sure glad you got here so fast, Detective."

"What is the problem, Chief?" Detective Dang asked his Boss.

The hard-faced, over weight cigar-puffing, chief of police, said, "Mrs. Applecrumby called 911 and my office, looking for *you*. She reported gunshots and that someone had stolen her—black diamond? Anyways, George was the first on the scene." The Chief then pointed toward a lamp a cushioned rocking chair where an officer was searching on his hands and knees for something or anything. "He found some strange activity you better check out."

George replied upon hearing his name. "She kept her diamond in a handmade, black, carved wooden security box that is also missing. Our units are canvassing the area inside and outside the complex for possible activities."

"Detective!" The Chief boomed over the noisy room. "Find the shooter and Mrs. A's property. Consider this a priority case and report your findings to me as soon as possible."

Chief turned his head to see if anyone was looking at him and the Detective, then continued, "I must leave and get Marge," the Chief's wife, "and our daughter who is performing in a local play.

Linda is playing *Betsy Ross* and tells the story of sewing the first American flag."

"Yes sir," Detective Dang said. He shook his head in amazement with a puzzled look on his face.

The detective paused for a moment, thinking. He began professionally scanning the crime scene observing everything in sight. He approached Mrs. A. sitting in an armchair after medical personnel had completed their medical examination and found her vital signs to be okay. She had been scared and fainted. She is now awake and a little nervous.

Dang was soft-spoken as he questioned the retired senior the Who, What, When, Where, and Why questions. Looking around the room, he then noticed a picture of a white cat on the corner table. Dang then wondered, *where is Fluffy?*

A police investigator approached the detective. "Sir, we cannot find any evidence of gunshots. We did observe a black box on the floor between a recliner and end table. We also found broken glass under the Christmas tree."

"Thank you," the detective replied.

The detective looked the sweet elderly grandma straight in the eyes. "Grandma, when did you put up the Christmas tree?"

"Yesterday, my sister and daughter came to decorate the Christmas tree. They did a beautiful job," she said.

The detective walked around the room, thinking, looking, and weighing the evidence. *Gunshots, Fluffy, new Christmas tree, broken glass, the black box next to a table and chair, and a missing black diamond. Wow!* He thought.

"Grandma, you were sitting in that recliner, the one next to the lamp, when you heard the gunshot?"

"Yes," she replied, "that is my favorite place to sit. I watch television, read, admire my memorabilia, look outside at the trees, and fall asleep in *my* chair."

"Ok." He paused. "You heard gunshots—then passed out.

You woke, could not find your black box and called 911, and Chief Hardy's office."

"Yes, exactly. That is what you told me to do if I ever had a problem. Now find my diamond and catch the person who took it, Detective," Mrs. A said.

Carefully, slowly, pointedly, the detective cast a sharp eye over the crime scene and under the Christmas tree, to the broken glass. The glass gleaming on the ground officers had determined to be a tree ornament.

The detective, talking to himself in a low toned voice, *"Fluffy was playing with the tree ornaments,"* he paused. *"She caused them to fall on the tile floor."* He paused, thinking again! *"The Christmas tree ornaments exploded? Sounds like gunshots?"*

Dang summoned an officer. "Go into the washroom, under the pantry, and find Fluffy." Then Detective Dang announced, "Fluffy had run away, scared!" A long pause, "Fluffy is our shooter!"

Mrs. A was excited to see the officer return holding *Fluffy*. The cat leaped out of the officer's arms and onto Mrs. A's lap.

Detective Dang walked to the recliner and end table. He turned on the lamp. With the light on he was able to see clearly and locate the beautiful carved black box under the end table. *Empty?!*

Let's see? Under the magazine rack, between the recliner and end table. The detective turned his attention to the recliner. He slid his hand along the opening between the armrest and seat. Feeling something substantial, he grabbed the object in his right-hand index finger and thumb. He moved toward the light and opened his hand.

In the palm of his hand, there was a large flat black stone cut in the shape of a diamond. He shook his head in amazement. "Mrs. A, is this the black diamond you were missing?"

"Yes, it is. Oh! Thank you," she said.

"This beautiful diamond was given to me, from you, when you were in the seventh grade. The artwork you did on the diamond is gorgeous. And, its inscription is so very precious to me."

A grandma's warm hugs and sweet memories.

She remembers all of your accomplishments

and forgets all of your mistakes. [18]

Barbara Cage

The detective again shook his head! This time in amusement.

Mrs. A. interrupted the detective, "Dang, look at what you inscribed on the side of the diamond."

Dang read the inscription to your Grandmother.

"Grandma, I love you, Dang."

Grandma A. sat in her favorite recliner and fell asleep. Dang cleared the house. Case Closed.

Soon after, like so many elderly, Mrs. Applecrumby relocated to a convalescent home.

Dave, who has lived here at VOP for many years chimed in, "Her name was Mille. I remember her and the diamond incident. It had both a happy and sad ending. She transferred to a convalescent home near the freeway. Unfortunately, she passed away soon after."

Bob said, "That is interesting, with a twist ending. It makes a Blind Man wonder how safe are we here, especially me, being blind?"

Bert interrupted saying, "I think we are safe here . . . most of the time?"

Although, one beautiful bright sunny morning while enjoying walking from the gym to the spa on the narrow walkway lined with VOP's choice of beautiful water conservative plants a short heavyset lady was walking toward the gym and me. I had seen her many times before using the gym equipment. I noted she does not acknowledge anyone when given even a kind or the pleasantest of hellos, good morning, or how are you. Most time when passed, she would turn away, look down at the ground and sometimes turn her back to you. On this occasion, entirely out of character she exposed a large, maybe eight-inch home-style kitchen knife on me! She pointed and poked the knife to me! She told me, "Stay away, or I will cut you!" She repeated several times. I stepped to the side, avoiding her threat allowing her the pathway to the gym where she walked on the gym's treadmill.

I recognized her distrusted attitude that caused me to worry and consider what could happen to me or others. I felt it was my duty to report the incident to the office and not dial 911. The management knew her and recorded the episode saying, "They will talk to her."

Maybe two days later the poor lady had a real meltdown? Did someone call 911? The police arrived at her apartment, where they found her locked inside. She was ranting vulgarities. She was saying things like "I will kill you. Go away, you pigs," and much worse.

Management and the police kept the people away from her for safety reasons. Her family or caregiver eventually was contacted, management told us. About 3 hours later, people were getting tired watching and started home or to their afternoon naps.

When her sister arrived, the lady calmed, and finally quieted down. She and her sister were escorted out of the building by the police.

Where she went, no one knows. The office had no comments. Her apartment became vacated, and shortly, it went up for rent.

"See we are safe," Bert said. A problem occurred, and was controlled professionally, I guess?

Changing back to the present and throughout this manuscript, Albie has asked repeatedly, "Do you like it here?" or "Why do you like it here?" And other similar subjects. Yes, we like it here. Does senior living have shortcomings? Yes, and we accept them. Maybe the following will enlighten a motive to stay here with the crazies on the patio, under the umbrella, with the Blind Man, a Big Man and other characters mentioned.

Days will get better. The past vanished and what happened will never reappear, except in memory, in pictures or by the written word — thousands of images stored in boxes and albums, while some favorites hang on the walls or stored in our mind. Many photos float somewhere in what is called 'I-cloud' which is generated by the computer, or a telephone camera—I guess?

Samaheito, a Buddhist monk from whom I learned many Buddhist ways, had traveled extensively. He has given lectures and visited other Buddhist temples around the world. One day I asked him a question, "In your travels, what or where, was the most interesting, famous or favorite place you've visited?"

To my surprise, he said. "Right here, with you—in this place, right now."

"Really, how and why is that?"

All material things are temporary. All things past are memories stored in our minds. Today is now and I cannot bring the past here. I look forward to tomorrow; good things and people like you, whom I meet and educate to the Buddhist ways . . . We as a species need a few things to survive such as food, clothing, shelter, sanitary items and medicine."

After my trip in which I learned from this monk, and returning to our home in the Santa Clarita Valley, my wife and I were excited to evaluate what we wanted in life—from that point on. Did we need, or did we not need, certain things we accumulated.

Just like other people over the years, we accumulate many material things. As we age, we become more medically-conscious and less material. Needing less the Mrs. and I committed to eliminating our material life. We will downsize to as little as possible. The boat and RV sold first. *Such memories they were!*

The garage and storage rooms were cleaned out. The older car sold. All the boy toys liquidated; gone but *how I miss them!* Our favorite imports accumulated from around the world, such as carved wooden cabinets, Ming Jars, small and big statues, and custom furniture—all sold. Many items transferred to the children for their use and care. Soon the house went up for sale and sold.

We moved here, into a senior living complex, eliminating many responsibilities. We indeed downsized from our 4,000 square foot home to a 1,000 square foot home. Why downsize as we did? No more house maintenance, mowing the lawn, climbing the stairs and less tax to mention a few. Today, we are happy—and free—to roam the world. We lock the door, get in the car, and drive. When we return, we unlock the door, regroup, and do it all over again. It's a beautiful life.

Standing in a *Do Not Disturb* corner is the fishing gear that calls out: *I'm ready, let's go fishing.* Equipment I cannot let go—yet! Cluttering the opposite corner, on the floor and in bookshelves, are writings and research papers for my published books. A prized collection of Buddha images, one of a kind carvings and favorite pictures are carefully placed in cabinets. The walls display favorite photos keeping the past alive.

On a recent trip to Thailand, the question surfaced, *what would you do if a community fire, flood, or high magnitude earthquake occurred at home?*

I know our lives would change! First, we would pray no one is hurt and that everyone quickly overcomes their fears and anxieties. As soon as possible we would call the children to confirm they are ok. Then we ask about our home. Our family's preplanned plan, if possible: the children will salvage what is left.

If we experienced a disaster or emergency evacuation, *what three things would we take?*

Married fifty plus years, the question: *What would a loving, sharing couple—believing in a 50/50 marriage—carry with them while slowly running or hobbling out the door?*

Each spouse will select one item; then together, we choose a third. Understand, we are older, and cannot carry many things. The beautiful, kind, loving, and straightforward wife will select her family's bronze bowl engraved with family genealogy and unique souvenirs.

Material me. The first thought would be the fishing gear, then consider it replaceable and leave it. In combination, grab a twelve hundred-year-old Buddha statue presented to me in 1965 by a Senior Monk from the order of Theravada Buddhism of Vietnam for work performed. The unique Buddha sits beside the Holy Bible passed down with my genealogy records inside. Grab them both and go.

The third, we will look at each other and, if necessary, skip the first two choices.

We will hold each other's hand, walk together, letting God guide us to safety.

Chapter??

Superstition

Tony Farentino

The Magic Cat, a Black Cat on Friday the 13th and a Full Moon?

What may be superstition to one person may not be to another. Fear is the lack-of-trust one has when not believing in an All-Mighty.

Does it become the poison to the delicate-minded? Does that mean our superstition is the ignorance of people and nations?

"We are all tattooed in our cradles with the beliefs of our tribes."[19]

Oliver Wendell Holmes

Is superstition the not knowing? Or is it ignorance?

"Ignorance breeds monsters to fill vacancies of the soul
That are unoccupied by the verities of knowledge." [20]

Horace Mann.

Superstition or ignorance? As I look around, I notice that we are all caught up in the beliefs of others. We are also caught up in our conclusions

Will Rogers summed it up,

"Everybody is ignorant, only on different subjects." [21]

I was walking with Mildred to the clubhouse mailbox. The conversation was the usual, "How are your aches and pains today?"

She replied, "Like so many others, some get better, and new ones startup."

"Interesting!" I said. "Mildred, I have an *unimportant* question for you? Do you have superstitions? Those you practice or that concern you?"

"Not really . . . Except, I don't like the number *thirteen*— especially *Friday the thirteenth*. Why?" She asked.

"I was just wondering? No reason! Most people I ask include or say a black cat when walking in front of them. Mildred, how about stepping on a crack in a sidewalk? You double-stepped over that crack behind you."

"No way! I did not. Did I? Did I, really?"

"Yes! You did. Don't worry! Nothing is going to happen except you may get unwanted mail in your mailbox. I hope you don't!"

One super-hot September day I finally arrived home. Inside I was sitting, enjoying ice tea with the air condition running. Outside two men moved a ladder to the center of my window that reached up to the second-story windows.

My phone rang. It was Guile, the Big Man, calling me. I answered, "Hello?"

"Silver Fox did you see or hear from the blind man today?"

"No, Johnny Gamboa and his Orchestra recording friend were coming over this morning. They possibly went to breakfast. Something they often do."

"That's strange. Bob wanted to go to central park and walk the trails. I guess we won't walk today!"

"Guess not today big guy!" I then placed the telephone receiver back in its cradle.

At that moment the window washer with wet shiny black hair, perspiring with sweat droplets, gawked at me through the window glass. Jose (his name tag indicated), the sweaty man, quickly removed the window screen. A second man pulled on a rope that extended a ladder to the second-floor window.

Once secured, he carried his water bucket and sponge up the ladder. The man on the ground washed his assigned window. When finished cleaning the hard-working fellow stepped back around the ladder to its opposite side. After walking behind the ladder, he prepared to clean the second dirty window.

I noticed he did not walk *under* the ladder. I called out and asked with a smile on my face, *"Superstitious?"*

"Yes," Jose is pointing up at the man on the ladder. "He dropped his bucket on me. The bucket full of water darn near knocked me out. I received five stitches in my head. See, right here!" He pointed to his hairline.

"How about Friday the Thirteenth, good or bad?" I asked.

"Not good. On Friday the thirteenth, a black cat crossed my path. At the same time, I stepped on a sidewalk crack and tripped— broke this arm," pointing at his deformed wrist.

> *"If a black cat crosses your path,*
>
> *It signifies that the animal is going somewhere."* [22]
>
> Groucho Marx

Is their superstition here at VOP? I think so. Did I want to investigate and get into its mysteries? No.

I leaned back in my comfortable chair. As the air condition labored, I fell asleep.

When I woke an hour later, I went directly to my laptop. Sometimes I think I am addicted to the computer. Aha! Never mind that.

I checked and found that the number thirteen is synonymous with bad luck. Many consider having thirteen guests at a party unlucky. Architects plan and design houses, factories, office buildings, and other structures without a 13th floor or number thirteen on their elevators. Most couples do not get married on the 13th. According to a leading real estate agent, not many homes are sold on the dreaded Friday the 13th.

Wikipedia: *The number thirteen dates back to Friday 13, 1307 when hundreds of Knights Templar, across France, were arrested and burned to death. (The Knights Templars were the elite fighting force of their day, highly trained, well-equipped and highly motivated; one of the tenets of their religious order— they were forbidden from retreating.)*

King Philip IV of France wanted to eliminate the Templars formed in 1100 AD by King Philippe I. King Philip wanted to create a new order of Knights, loyal only to him.

On Friday, October 13th, 1307, King Philip IV of France ordered all Templars to be rounded up and thrown in prison. The Knights were accused of numerous crimes including heresy, treason, and burned unmercifully to death. [23]

"Too many kings can ruin an army." [24]

Homer

There have been some recent disasters associated with 13. California, The *Ferguson Fire* started on a Friday night, July 13, 2018, at 9:36 PM in the South Fork Merced River drainage in the Sierra National Forest. Records recorded the fire started from the vehicles defective catalytic converter. The fire burned 96,901 acres. The fire fully contained 22 August 2018.

November 13, 2008, the *Tea Fire* started at the historic *Tea House,* a landmark building near Montecito in Santa Barbara County, California. The fire destroyed 210 homes.

Californians, in the United States, must all be unlucky? Their Constitution, after all, was adopted on November 13, 1849.

A Superstition? GOOD solution—November 13th, 1956, the United States Supreme Court ruled racial segregation on public buses unconstitutional. We now fly, ride trains, cars, and buses without splitting them in half.

Happy Birthday? Is it unlucky to be born on the thirteenth day of a month? No! I do not think so.

Many people would have you believe it is an unlucky number. Again, it is not!

It's written if you were born or expecting a newborn on the 13th of the month you have something GOOD to look forward to. You have a great love of family. Tradition indicates you are at peace with nature.

You are strongly disciplined and approach life with a blend of practicality and creativity. We need more people born on the thirteenth.

There are many celebrities and personalities born on the 13th day of a month. Some of those birthday babies include **Marie Osmond**, 1959, an American singer, born in Ogden, Utah. **Mary-Kate Olsen and Ashley Olsen,** American fashion designers and former child actresses; Also known as the Olsen twins. **Samuel Beckett**, playwright. Former President of Cuba, **Fidel Castro. Ellen Burse** identified as **Elizabeth Winemakers**, TV hostess, born in Rotterdam, Netherlands. **Beverly Johnson,** an American model and actress (Ashanti Land of No Mercy), born in Buffalo, New York. **Chris Carter**, born in Bellflower, California, 1956 aspired to an American television producer (The X-Files) and many other productions. Are these people unlucky? I do not think so.

There are many non-celebrities born on the thirteenth. My stepmother and her first son were two of those people. She lived a long life. He was a career enlisted military man.

Superstitions, where do we go from here?

Let's be clear, for him Friday the 13th held no fear. He wasn't superstitious (or even a little bit stitious), and didn't view the day as particularly suspicious, or with the promise of the unpropitious.

It was then a black cat crossed his path, causing him to step on a crack which made him stagger under a ladder and shatter a mirror being transported by a passing albatross, who suffered fatal blood loss from a shard which flew hard into

its heart. [25]

Brian Bilston, Bad Luck, 2015

So why do we fear 13 or Friday the 13th, other than that horror movie with the same name? The National Geographic reports one theory. The trepidation (fear and anxiety) surrounding Friday the 13th is rooted in religious beliefs. The 13th guest at the Last Supper—Judas, the apostle, said to have betrayed Jesus—and the crucifixion of Jesus on a Friday. The two elements put together—13 and Friday—create one seemingly inauspicious day. Then there is always Friday 13, XX13? Oh, my, gosh! What shall we do?

That's enough!

I cannot take it anymore!

Let's turn the page and wrap it up.

Chapter 14

It's a wrap

*M*any, if not most, seniors have expressed, "It has been a good life with its ups and downs." They, the seniors and I generally say, "At the end of the day this last year has been full of new experiences. The months have been fulfilling, the weeks interesting, and the days mysterious." Then we wonder what will tomorrow bring?

> *In all things of nature,*
> *There is something of the marvelous." [26]*
>
> Aristotle

Several new residents have moved into VOP. Others have moved out to comparable living centers, and others have passed on.

VOP management has helped make life more interesting for many. Every month there are different planned entertainment events. There is a scheduled *Pizza Day*, Bingo, Keno, as well as summer parties. Holiday party days include Valentine day, Thanksgiving, and Christmas.

Management generally provides transportation to various markets, breakfast or dinner locations at local cafés.

Karaoke—people enjoy singing their favorite songs. Mine? Tennessee Ernie Ford's version of 'Sixteen Tons,' initially written by Merle Travis—about a coal miner from Kentucky. It was first recorded in Hollywood, California, on August 8, 1946, and released in July 1947, by Capitol Records on Travis's album: *Folk Songs of the Hills.* This song, 'Sixteen Tons, helped the albums collection become a gold record.

The version recorded by Tennessee Ernie Ford reached number one on the Billboard charts in 1955. Another version by Frankie Laine, 1956, was released in Western Europe which gave Ford's version some competition.

Then there is the 1:30-3 PM *Wine and Cheese* social. Participants enjoy tasting different brands of wine from around the world. Should I say, different local stores? Many do not understand the many different types, or qualities, of the wines. Just let me drink!

Some joke, "Where's the *Ripple?*" The seniors are referring to a ninety-nine cent bottle of fortified, lightly-carbonated, sweet wine purchased in the soda section of local grocery stores, last sold *in 1960.* Even sixteen-year-olds could buy Ripple at the time. Others want their *Thunderbird* wine or discontinued *Night Train.* What's important is that most guests enjoy themselves developing some excellent social skills. Others get irritated at themselves and make an ass of a good situation. Most say, "Eat, drink, and be merry before inebriation." Then the good old seniors go home for an afternoon nap.

Yes! I almost forgot. There is the once a month birthday party social. Everyone is welcome to come and sing "Happy Birthday" to *themselves* ….

This year was a first—an outstanding presentation presented to its guests in the VOP clubhouse. The program titled, *"A Christmas Concert,"* produced by Robert Seijas, the Blind Man. His best friend of sixty years performed: Johnny Gamboa, accompanied by his international orchestra, entertainers, and recording artist.

Johnny, master of ceremony and singer of his five-piece orchestra, was incredible. He sang several oldies — everyone's favorite *New York, New York,* and a variety of Christmas songs that included *Jingle Bells,* and *White Christmas.*

My artist of choice was Arut Gotcha. He played a 3000-year-old instrument called Oud. The Oud is a short-neck lute pear-shaped, stringed instrument with 11 or 13 strings grouped in 5 or 6 courses. The Oud is iconic within the Middle East and North African countries. The Oud is known as *The King of Instruments.*

Robert presented some humor to the program reciting stories of comedy. Remember the *Hickory Dickory Doc* story presented in an earlier chapter? Everyone enjoyed his more extended version.

Johnny, as a standup comedian was super. One true story he did tell us:

Bob Hope, the Teacher.

"Hi, I know you," Bob Hope pointed at Johnny.

Johnny, a Latino, replies to Bob Hope, "Were you ever in Jail?"

"Oh? Yes! I remember. You opened for Johnny Cash and me at the Indiana State Fair."

"Yes, in front of 5,000 screaming fans," Johnny replied.

Bob Hope, (1903-2003) an American stand-up comedian, vaudevillian, actor, singer, dancer, athlete, and author with a career that spanned nearly 80 years, [26.1]

Bob looked deep into Johnny's eyes. In a soft-spoken voice, very politely said, "Johnny, you should stick to your instruments and singing, that which you are good at." He shifted his eyebrows up and whispered from behind his trademark smile, "You stick to singing, and I do the comedy. Ok?"

"Yes, Sir!" And they both laughed. The crowd came to life with laughter.

****

Bob Hope and Johnny talked about his next USO Christmas gig, shook hands, and then departed their separate ways.

Johnny announced, "Today, we have two special guests— first, Suzanne Lodge, singer, dancer, and actress. One of her many credits is dancing with Elvis Presley in the 1965 movie *Spinout*, by MGM productions.

"The second announcement," Johnny continued, "Gary, known as the *Silver Fox*, it's his Birthday today! He is turning 78 but only looks 60! Congratulations! He is retired and lives here, with all of you. He is a good friend and helper to Robert, my friend."

Happy Birthday, Gary. He deserves a standing ovation, with a drum roll!"

I received both drum roll and standing ovation what a surprise!

What a birthday bash. It started with a four dollar breakfast, light gym workout, some shopping, lunch with friends, a short nap and a concert. Then off to where my family gave me a birthday party and dinner. What a runaway day!

To get this far, you must have a sense of humor and wit. Reading this hodge-podge of stories I hope has been thought-provoking.

Congratulations!

It was said,

Those who put their lives to understand

They do not have to organize other people's life.

Live, and let others live to smile and laugh. [27]

Unknown.

The most challenging journey of a writer is always the start. The start is the first word, a single word. I made that first step and did not regret writing *The Blind Man, Big Man, and Silver Fox.*

It is one of the blessings of old friends,

You can afford to be stupid with them. [28]

Ralph Waldo Emerson

As they say, *old dog's new tricks?* Samuel, Sam—60 something—his last name unknown, has moved on. His shared rents with another were too costly. He often said, "To save money, I should move to Mexico." Finally, he did! Shortly after arriving in his new country, Sam telephoned and bragged about his little apartment on the beach. He enjoys the hot weather, *Maria, Rita,* and Margaritas on the beach under the palm trees. Sam now brags, a pack of cigarettes costs fifty cents. Do we think *he possibly drinks too much?* Yes as long as it belongs to someone else.

He called Laura on another occasion and invited her to join him in Mexico. She told us, "He is a crazy lunatic, and I hung up the telephone on him." No one has heard from Sam since.

Albie, Albert—the 80-plus-year-old colorful senior whose catchphrase: *"Do You like It Here?"* moved to California's VOP after retirement to be closer to their children and grandchildren, Albie and Lois miss the theaters of New York. Together they have seen many of the top broadways plays. He recites and explains different stage plays or acts to use on the patio under the umbrella. He also continues to visit local theaters in Hollywood—for the art, performances, and to relax. But, Albie continues, and may never stop asking the question, "Do you like it here?"

Guillermo, 58, The Big Man, The Refrigerator, jokes and shares his humor and wit. If you want to know anything about Sylmar or the San Fernando Valley and the surrounding area, he is the person to ask. Guillermo has a 'medical retirement' which requires his wife Judy to continue working. He does, however, continue to cater to private parties upon request. The Spice Girl and Sauce were from his time spent daydreaming.

Bob, Robert, The Blind Man, is an exciting guy. He has been officially blind for ten years. The stories in this book relating to Bob are factual, to the best of his recollection. He is improving his piano and song music daily, and his application request for help with the Veterans Affair is beginning to help his situation. Bob is very upbeat with his blind circumstances.

The Silver Fox salutes Bob and the Blind.

Me? I'm Gary Popejoy, 78, also known as the Silver Fox— retired. Today as an author, I have written two books. I also have two books on hold until I finish writing the one you are reading: *The Blind Man, Big Man, and Silver Fox*.

I was once asked, "Did you ever make mistakes, especially the same one over and over?" I am proud to say, "I never did and proud of it."

The truth is (snickering to myself), I never made the same blunder mistakes *twice*. I made them *five* or *six* times, or until I understood. Once I get it right, I find it's time to make changes.

> *Writing is like driving at night in the fog.*
>
> *You can only see as far as your headlights,*
>
> *But you can make the whole trip that way. [29]*
>
> E.L. Doctorow

I want to leave you with this observation from a time when I was walking in a forest in Asia. I called it *Beauty in its Splendor:*

Beauty in its splendor

Walk the country road, "Exercise is good," the doctor said.

"It's cool."

What will I see, beauty and its splendor,

Wild and open?

Meditate the journey and exercise along the way,

Enjoy!

The air is still and fresh from the night;

The sun is rising.

Quiet, bright, and beautiful is the sunrise,

Feels good.

Above the tall forest, no clouds in sight,

A hot day is coming!

Alone on the country road, Beautiful sights to see.

Great teakwood trees grow in the field,

Looks like a forest.

Sugarcane is ten feet tall, on the right,

Rice fields on the left.

The paved road stops, the dirt road begins.

'Keep on walking.'

No water in the aqueduct to feed the fields, '

Wonder why?'

Four months of the rainy season is over,

Keep on walking!

Alone on the road, I hear the wind, a breeze,

I see it flutter the leaves.

Chanting and musical instruments, in the distance,

A celebration.

Dewdrops from the leaves, land on the shoulder,

Dirty shirt

A dog barks protecting his property,

Move on.

Charcoal burning smells the air, someone prepares a daily meal.

Mother with child on a motorcycle, going to school,

They wave.

Deepwater pool, man fishing,

Motorbike beside.

Wildflowers bloom in red, white, yellow;

The aroma clears the head.

Tall trees; coconut, banana, and papaya all grow fruit,

Want to eat.

Halfway I see, had better turn back,

Dusty trail.

What will I see? The front side of beauty,

The backside of

Splendor.

Beauty in reverse, hot sun, walk, enjoy,

Healthy too.

Can't wait for tomorrow to see it again,

I hope it does not rain.

Write it down, do not let it escape, read tomorrow, what you see today.

Tomorrow, do it again.

It has been a long road to this point. Sharing these words with you has been fun. I want to leave you with -----

There is one thing worse than the hardness of a stone-cold heart, that is, the softness of a big head. I feel one needs to show concern for the suffering seniors or misfortunes of them and others. Compassion is not promising them a bridge that crosses a nonexistent river they do not need. Interaction and helping them, the depressed, when required, is compassion.

Be kind and listen to the needs of others.

Silver Fox

Until next time?

Gary Popejoy

Join Someone

Under an Umbrella on a Patio

The Author

Throughout his life, Gary Popejoy has explored many points on the North American continent and multiple countries in Europe and Asia. Gary is a U.S. Army veteran from the Vietnam era. He then joined Air America fighting with the CIA in the secret war of Laos. He explored Buddhist temples and received Buddha images, which he is most proud.

While a manager at Air America, a former civilian airline operated by the CIA, he visited many Buddhist temples, photographing and interacting with monks. Gary then became production manager at Lockheed's famous *Skunk Works*, where the F-117 Nighthawk stealth attack aircraft, SR-71 Blackbird strategic reconnaissance aircraft, and TR-1/U-2 programs developed.

A resident of Santa Clarita, California, Gary has been a business owner, community volunteer, president of Mad about Rising Crime (MARC), and associated to the Santa Clarita Sheriff Departments Anti-Gang Task Force.

Currently, Gary is a writer/author and member of the *Golden Pen Writers Guild*. He has contributed to several of their published anthologies.

Contact Gary at www.garypopejoy.com or www.garypopejoy.weebly.com and Amazon.com

Book Titles

Author Gary Popejoy
MELTDOWN
The Disappearing Glaciers *(2017)*
****

BUDDHA AND HIS TEMPLES
Fifteen in 37 Kilometers (2018)
*****

Coming Soon
Buddha, His Teachings from Birth to Death and Beyond (2020)
Buddha, Meditation and Seven days of Buddha (2020/21)
As a member of the Golden Pen Writers' Guild Gary has
contributed to the following published anthologies.
Waiting at the Train Station
Crossroads, Turning Point, and Defining Moments (2015)
The Language of Love
A Collection of Poetry, Prose, and Stories from the Heart (2016)

Writing Out Loud

Exploring Relationships in Prose and Poetry (2016)

Imaginings

A Golden Pen Anthology (2018)

And

This and That (2019)

Find them at Amazon.com and Garypopejoy.weebly.com

Author's Last Page

The Blind Man, Big Man and Silver Fox have something for everyone; adventure, gossip, humor, mystery, and romance. These are stories and observations from seniors who live the part.

Does it have both personal truth and little white lies…?

Look inside!

These are compelling stories from many chats with seniors while sitting at a patio table under an umbrella in a senior living center. A Blind Person, Bob, and a Cook, Guillermo, encouraged Author Gary Popejoy and his works: *Meltdown, the Disappearing Glaciers,* and *Buddha and His Temples, Fifteen in 37 Kilometers* to create an exciting book of life for fifty-five year old and older seniors. This book was molded from inception using stories contributed from people of various backgrounds. The rich stories evolve into a humorous tome.

The Blind Man, Big Man and Silver Fox are a pack of three from different economic and social situations who practice fellowship. The three guys sit sipping wine, diet soda, eating cheese and crackers barbecuing hotdogs, and reminiscing. They hope to open senior's eyes about themselves and others to bring a humorous laugh. Youth to fifty-five year old will gain insight into what is coming in later life.

At work

Author Gary Popejoy; The Blind Man, Big Man and Silver Fox
take notes for his next book:

Buddha's Teachings, From Life to Death

and Beyond

Advertisement

Del Prado Estates

The Blind Man, Big Man and the Silver Fox wants to say Thank You; Del Prado Estates, for being a sponsor.

Del Prado Estates is your modern-retro home away from home. Window walls stretch across the living room, master bedroom, family room, and office. The open view allows for an incredible view overlooking the Naches River Valley and nearby mountains. Splash right into the heated indoor pool from the diving board or slide! If that's not enough fun, head downstairs via the elevator to enjoy the spacious family room. Step outside for a marvelous view and into the relaxation of warmth in a large spa. Enjoy and have the time of your life at this beautiful, accommodating, one-of-a-kind home!

https://www.airbnb.com/rooms/21728349

Notes

[1]   Stephen   King – You can't deny laughter;
https://www.goodreads.com/quotes/46051-you-can-t-deny-laughter-when-itcomes-it-.

[2]   Spanish proverb – Gossip Those who gossip to you will gossip about you
https://www.google.com/url?sa=i&source=images&cd=&ved=0ahUKE
wiQq57_PfAhVJvKwKHee5DisQMwhSKBMwEw&url=https%3A%2F
%2Fwww.wow4u.com%2Fgossip%2F&psig=AOvVaw3Lb-:
http://www.scholarship.org/clientuploads/MMM10.30.17.pdf

Chapter 1:

[3]   Quite Walter Bagehot - An inability to stay quiet is one offered the. - Brainy
Quote https://www.brainyquote.com/quotes/walter_bagehot_122634

Chapter 3:

[4]   *'This and that'* rewritten from writing by Raymond O'Connor of the Golden
Pen Writers Guilt, with permission.

Chapter 4:

[5] Lisa Minnelli Quotes – Brainy quote,
https://www.brainyquote.com/quotes/liza_minnelli_470928 (accessed January 15,
2019).

Chapter 5: 6:

https://www.google.com/url?sa=i&source=images&cd=&ved=0ahUKEwiQq5
uT7_PfAhVJvKwKHee5DisQMwhSKBMwEw&URL=https%3A%2F%2Fwww.
wow4u.com%2Fgossip%2F&psig=AOvVaw3Lb-

[6]   French Journalist Antoine Rivarol quoted;
https://www.brainyquote.com/quotes/a ntoine_rivarol_126514

[7]   Quotes by Dr. James G. Bilkey –   Forbes;
https://www.forbes.com/quotes/2263/

[8][8.1]   The   Triple-filter   Test   –   Inspiration   Peak,
http://www.inspirationpeak.com/cgi-bin/stories.cgi?record=150   (accessed

January15,2019).ThetriplefilterTestttp://www.inspirationpeak.com/cgibin/stories.cgi?record=150 (located March 23, 2019).

Chapter 7:

[9]   Joaquin   Miller;   https://www.azquotes.com/author/65314-Joaquin_Miller Chapter 8:

[10]   The   Blind   Girl.   Author   Unknown;   Get   apps   at https://play.google.com/store/apps/details?id=com.thanhcs.motivationstories.
           The 10   Best Inspirational Short   Stories   (updated   2019 .., https://wealthygorilla.com/10-most-inspirational-short-stories/ (accessed March 23, 2019).

Chapter 9:

[11]   Detroit   City,   Bobby   Bare; https://www.google.com/search?rlz=1C1CHBD_enTH774TH774&q=tom+jones+detroit+city&stick=H4sIAAAAAAAAAONgFuLRT9c3LDTNSjE2NjVVgvGScgoLTLW0spOt9HNLizOT9YtSk_OLUjLz0uOTc0qLS1KLrPJLMlKLFMpSi4oz8_OKAXDldLtKAAAA&sa=X&ved=2ahUKEwjA8p_XkPvfAhUEOq0KHXHqAEMQri4wCXoECAgQKQ&biw=680&bih=640

[12]Love; http://quotepixel.com/picture/love/anonymous/if_there_is_anything_better_than_to_be_loved_it_is_loving

Chapter 10:

[13]   Dr.Seuss;https://www.pinterest.com/pin/565272190701086178/

[14]   [14.1]   Corey Ford, American writer; https://www.pinterest.com/pin/504403226988221405

[14.2]   This story is rewritten from a story by William Tozzi, "What Does He Want From   Me   Now?"(2018)   of   the   Golden   Pen   Writers   Guilt,   with permission.wtozzi@ix.netcom.com

Chapter 11:

[15]   Eleanor Roosevelt   - | https://pocketsergeant.files.wordpress.com/2015/11/wpid-5cd8c7fb-2.jpg

[16]   *PTSD,* Post-Traumatic Stress Disorder, is a **disorder** that develops in some people who have experienced a shocking, scary, or dangerous event.

Chapter 12:

[17]   Ocean,   up   and   down;   https://www.brainyquote.com/topics/ocean
https://www.lifehack.org/articles/communication/life-like-the-ocean-
cancalm.html

[18] Barbra Cage: https://www.scrapbook.com/poems/doc/23407.html

Chapter 13

[19] Oliver Wendell Holmes-We Are All Tattooed in Our Cradles with the Beliefs
     of   Our   ..,   https://www.newtownbee.com/we-are-all-tattooed-in-our-
     cradleswith-the-beliefs-o (accessed January 15, 2019).
     [20] Quote   by   Horace   Mann:
ttps://www.brainyquote.com/authors/horace_mann

     [21] Will   Rogers:

ttps://scholarsarchive.byu.edu/cgi/viewcontent.cgi?article=4126&context=byus q

[22]   Groucho Marx: https://www.goodreads.com/quotes/190471-if-a-black-
         catcrosses-your-path-it-signifies-that

[23]   The Knights Templar & Friday The 13th | The Knights Templar,
         http://www.theknightstemplar.org/friday/ (accessed January 15, 2019).

[24]   Quote   by   Homer: "Too   many   kings   …"   -
https://www.goodreads.com/quotes/645086-too-many-kings-can-ruin-

[25]   Friday   the   Thirteenth | Brian   Bilston's   Poe   Laboratory   try,
         https://brianbilston.com/2015/02/13/friday-the-thirteenth/   (accessed
         January 15, 2019)

Chapter 14

[26]   Aristotle-In   All   Things   of   Nature   There   is   Something   of..,
         https://www.brainyquote.com/quotes/aristotle_163785   (accessed
         January   15,   2019).   Aristotle   Quotes   -   Brainy   quote,
         https://www.brainyquote.com/quotes/aristotle_163785 (accessed March
         23, 2019).

[26.1] Bob Hope - Wikipedia, https://en.wikipedia.org/wiki/Bob_Hope (accessed
March 23, 2019).

[27]   Instant Quotation Dictionary, Donald O. Bolander, Career Institute (1972)
         555 E. Lang St Mundelein, Ill. 60060, Author Unknown.

[28]   Ralph Waldo Emerson; Instant Quotation Dictionary, Donald O.. Bolander, Career Institute (1972) 555 E. Lang St Mundelein, Ill. 60060

[29]   E. L. Doctorow Quotes; https://quotefancy.com/e-l-doctorow-quotes. : E.
L. Doctorow Quotes - Famous Quotes at Brainy quote, https://www.brainyquote.com/quotes/e_l_doctorow_389140 (accessed March 23, 2019).

[30] Footprints in the sand…; https://me.me/i/you-cant-leave-footprints-in-thesands-of-time-if-19300282, Author Unknown.

The end

www.ingramcontent.com/pod-product-compliance
Lightning Source LLC
Chambersburg PA
CBHW061513050726
47593CB00002B/548